LAUREL-LEAF
BOOKS

U
lexile 890

"No group should have veto power over what books we can read," Barney volunteered.

"Exactly." The librarian nodded her head. "Think, Kate. If *Huckleberry Finn* is going to be thrown out of school because it offends some black parents, what's to stop other groups of parents from getting up *their* lists of books they want out of here? Catholics, Jews, feminists, antifeminists, conservatives, liberals, Greeks, Turks, Armenians. Where does it end, Kate?"

NAT HENTOFF is a well-known staff writer for *The Village Voice*. He is the author of *Jazz Country, I'm Really Dragged but Nothing Gets Me Down, This School Is Driving Me Crazy,* and *Does This School Have Capital Punishment?*.

ALSO AVAILABLE IN LAUREL-LEAF BOOKS:

YEARLING BOOKS are designed especially to entertain and enlighten young people. Patricia Reilly Giff, consultant to this series, received her bachelor's degree from Marymount College and a master's degree in history from St. John's University. She holds a Professional Diploma in Reading and a Doctorate of Humane Letters from Hofstra University. She was a teacher and reading consultant for many years, and is the author of numerous books for young readers.

The Day They Came to Arrest the Book

A Novel by
NAT HENTOFF

Published by
Dell Laurel-Leaf
an imprint of
Random House Children's Books
a division of Random House, Inc.
1540 Broadway
New York, New York 10036

The trademark Laurel-Leaf Library® is registered in the U.S.
Patent and Trademark Office.
The trademark Dell® is registered in the U.S. Patent and
Trademark Office.

Visit us on the Web! www.randomhouse.com/teens

Educators and librarians, for a variety of teaching tools,
visit us at www.randomhouse.com/teachers

ISBN: 0-440-91814-6

RL: 6.2

Reprinted by arrangement with Delacorte Press

Printed in the United States of America

August 1983

OPM 31 30

FOR
KATHY RUSSELL, IRENE TURIN,
SUSAN MAASZ, AND JUDITH KRUG

I

"He's going to be right inside the door," Luke said to Barney as they neared the entrance to George Mason High School. "He's going to be standing there with that big phony smile and that chocolate voice."

Luke, sticking out his stomach as far as a lean sixteen-year-old could, deepened his voice in imitation of the man behind the door—Michael Moore, also known as Mighty Mike, the principal of the school. " 'Welcome back, Luke, good buddy. Have a good summer? Yeah, you look like you had a great summer. Raring to get at the books, good buddy? Har, har, har, I *bet* you are.' "

Turning to Barney, who was shorter, a year older, and the incoming editor of the *George Mason Standard,* Luke said, "Why don't we go in the back way?"

Barney laughed. "He'll get us sooner or later. Might as well be now."

As they reached the front door, Barney opened it

and gestured for Luke to precede him. "After you, good buddy."

Luke scowled, poked his head in, and stiffened as a large man in his late forties, with a magnificent mane of prematurely white hair, fixed his pale-blue eyes on the boy. "Well, look who's here." Mr. Moore placed his hand on Luke's shoulder. "Cool Hand Luke. Have a good summer, good buddy?"

"I got possessed," Luke said tonelessly. "Somebody else is inside me now."

"Har, har, har." The principal dug his hand into the boy's shoulder. "Well, I hope *he* gets his papers in on time. Look who else is raring to get at the books. And at the *news*! Barnaby, you look like you had a great summer. That still is you, isn't it, Barnaby?"

"We switch," Barney said solemnly. "Sometimes what's in Luke gets into me."

"That's nothing new." The principal clapped Barney on the back. "Well, look who's here." Mr. Moore moved in on a group of students who had just opened the door. "Have a good summer, good buddy?"

"Let's *move*," Luke whispered to Barney. "He could do it all over again."

"I'm going in the library," Barney said. "I want to say hello to Mrs. Salters."

"Mrs. Salters, she's gone," said a cool, clipped voice behind them. "Checked out for good."

Barney turned. "Hey, Kate!" he said to the thin, crisp girl with jet-black hair and large round glasses. "You were supposed to write me this summer."

"I started to a couple of times"—Kate smiled—"but it was all so boring. Except for Mrs. Salters, and I didn't want to spoil your summer."

"What happened to her?"

"Well," said Kate, "she told my mother—you know, my mother went to college with her—that if she stayed another year, she'd kill him. She'd take a butcher knife, march right into his office, and cut out his tin heart. It was either murder or quit. So she quit."

"Who?" Barney and Luke asked in unison. "Who was she going to murder?"

"That yo-yo over there," Kate said impatiently, pointing to Mr. Moore, who waved cheerily back at her.

"Why? What did he do?" Barney asked.

Kate shook her head. "I don't know. That's all I heard. My mother was telling the story to my father until they realized I'd come into the room. She said she couldn't tell me the details, because if the story got spread all over school, that yo-yo would make it hard for Mrs. Salters to get another job."

"You don't know *anything* more?" Barney shouted.

"Summer's *over!*" the principal shouted from across the lobby. "Keep it down!" He grinned at them.

"Nothing," Kate whispered.

"Who's the new librarian?" Barney said glumly.

"Fitzgerald." Kate looked at her watch. "Something Fitzgerald. My mother says she feels sorry for her."

Deirdre Fitzgerald looked around the library that morning with satisfaction. It was all so inviting. The boldly colored posters, the newly polished tables (she'd done the polishing), the parade of magazines in the racks, and the books. Ah, the shelves and shelves and shelves of books.

Tall, slender, with long, lustrous brown hair and sharp features that might have been forbidding had her eyes and voice not been so soft, Deirdre walked along the shelves, opening books at random, reading a paragraph or two, and then putting them carefully back.

Stopping at her desk, she stood in reflection, remembering the day—she was sure it had been a Friday—when, as a little girl, she had gotten her first card at the public library branch near her home. She could still feel the excitement. And the delicious frustration. Would she ever be able to read all the books in that astonishingly clean, bright, orderly room? The white-haired librarian had laughed and said, "Don't count, Deirdre. It's not a contest. Enjoy them one at a time."

But she had counted, and indeed she had read a rather enormous number of the books in that library. As a child she had wanted to stay there all her life. And in a way—Deirdre Fitzgerald smiled—she had.

"My, you're in good spirits." A brisk, chunky blond woman in her early forties came into the library. "I feel like the bad fairy at the christening."

The librarian, frowning in puzzlement, looked at her. "I'm Deirdre Fitzgerald."

"Sorry, no manners. Me, I mean," said the blond woman. "When I've got something on my mind, I have no manners. I'm Nora Baines. I teach history in this amusement park. We'll be working together a lot because I am notorious among students for insisting that supplementary reading lists be taken seriously."

Deirdre motioned for Nora Baines to take a seat.

"No, thanks," said the history teacher. "I don't like to get too comfortable in this school. Makes it easier for them to ambush you."

"Them?"

"Everybody. Students. Fellow faculty members. Mighty Mike Moore, our magnetic principal. Parents. And various other citizens who consider public education to be the public's business. They're right, of course. It is the public's business. Still, I wish they'd all take a long sabbatical and keep their noses out of our affairs for a while. God, what a time we had last year."

"I heard something about a little trouble last year," Deirdre Fitzgerald said, "but Mr. Moore told me that it was just that—a few complaints about library books and textbooks, and they were all resolved okay."

"Ha!" Nora Baines snapped. "You'll see how he resolves complaints. That's why Karen Salters left. Listen, I've got to get to first period. We'll talk later. You need a crash course in how to survive around here. Hey, you a fighter?"

Deirdre smiled. "Only when my back is against the wall. Then I'm so terrifying, I scare even myself."

"Good," said Nora Baines from the door. "You don't know it yet, but that's exactly where your back is."

II

"This is a history course." Nora Baines was speaking, later that morning, with her customary staccato energy. "But we shall also be reading novels. Why do you suppose that is?"

"Because fiction," Barney said, "is sometimes more real than fact. I mean, it can tell you more than facts. It can tell you more about what ordinary people were like in certain times and places than laws and battles and things like that."

Nora Baines peered at Barney. "And why is that?"

"Well, because fiction is imagination. The novelist can suppose, and so he can get inside people's heads. Like, if he's writing about the past, and he knows a lot about the past, he makes you become part of it because you get all involved with the story and the people in it."

"He. He. He." Kate turned around and said dryly to Barney, "All novelists are males?"

"I expect Barney is willing to agree," said Nora Baines, "that his use of 'he' encompasses women as well."

Barney nodded in genial agreement.

"Why can't he say *she* then"—Kate turned back to the teacher—"and agree that 'she' encompasses men as well?"

"Because it doesn't feel right," Barney said.

"Uh-huh!" Kate's voice was triumphant. "Sure, sexism is comfortable, just as racism is. Why change when you're on top?"

Luke and some of the other boys guffawed.

"I didn't mean it like that," Kate said angrily, "and you know I didn't. Bunch of yo-yos."

"Kate has just made her point." Nora Baines looked at Luke. "That was such a comfortable bray, Luke Hagstrom. You will be right at home in our journey through the nineteenth century—until you meet Susan B. Anthony. She'll give you a good shaking up.

"Now"—Nora Baines was pacing in front of her desk —"about 'he' and 'she' and all that. You can avoid the pronouns, Kate, by using 'novelist' or 'writer' instead of 'he' in what Barney just said. For instance, 'If it's about the past, the novelist makes you become part of it.'

"As for myself," the history teacher went on, "I don't have any problem using 'he' to mean both genders because I grew up that way. I have certainly always considered myself part of mankind, after all. But I

understand what you're talking about, Kate. Just watch
out that you don't fall into such deformities of language
as 'clergyperson' or 'policeperson' or 'chairperson.' I
will not accept any such genderless abominations in any
paper in this class."

"The newspaper said last night," Luke volunteered
brightly, "that Mr. Moore is the new *chair* of the state
principals' association."

"He can't stand any more upholstering than he already has," said a voice from the back of the room.

"Ridiculous!" Nora Baines sat down with a thump.
"All right, let's get on with nineteenth-century American history. Your first assignment, as you can see by the
reading list, will be the numbered pages in Alexis de
Tocqueville's *Democracy in America*. He was a young
French nobleman who came here in 1831 to find out
what this young country was all about. And one of the
things he found was that this was no fake democracy.
The people really did rule. Or, as he put it, in America,
'The people are the cause and the aim of all things;
everything comes from them, and everything is absorbed
in them.' "

Kate snorted. "Male, white people did all the ruling.
Period."

"Patience," Nora Baines said. "You and Frederick
Douglass will get your chance. If I may continue, this
young Frenchman was worried, though. Even with all
this democracy, something seemed to be missing. What
do you suppose it was?"

Silence. Finally broken by Barney. "Well, it has to be what Kate said—only white males shared in that democracy."

"That is obvious to some of us now," Nora Baines said. "But what dangerous weakness in the new America did de Tocqueville see *then*?"

All faces were blank. The teacher sighed and said, "De Tocqueville was worried that *individual* differences were getting blurred in this grand rule by the people. Here—" She picked up a paperback book. "He wrote: 'Every citizen, being assimilated to all the rest, is lost in the crowd, and nothing stands conspicuous but the great and imposing image of the people at large.' "

There was still puzzlement among the students.

"Okay." Nora Baines got up and started pacing again. "Just a short time before, a revolutionary war had been fought to get rid of British tyranny. But now, was there a danger that the democratic majority could be as tyrannical as a king? Mind you, this young Frenchman admired a lot about America, but he also wrote: 'I know of no country in which there is so little independence of mind and real freedom of discussion as in America.' Do you see? He was afraid that individual freedom of thought was being lost in that great democratic crowd. It was one thing to dissent against the British in 1776, but by 1831 de Tocqueville found very few Americans who dared to dissent publicly against popular opinion in this new nation."

"That's crazy," Luke Hagstrom said. "Americans

have always been disagreeing with each other about all kinds of things. Look at the Abolitionists. Look at the Civil War, for God's sake. Look at the Vietnam War. Just listen to all those people calling in on the radio talk shows all the time—biting each other's heads off."

"I don't think it's as simple as Luke says," Barney broke in. "There are a lot of places in this country, and I bet there always have been, where if you're all alone in what you think, and you say what you think, you get treated like a leper or a criminal."

"Well, sure," Luke said, "if you let them do that to you. I just wouldn't *talk* to people that dumb."

"Great," said Kate. "That'd really help get your ideas across."

"Is it possible that both Luke and Barney are right?" Nora Baines asked. "Think about it as you read de Tocqueville. By the way, does everyone have a reading list?"

All nodded.

"*Democracy in America,*" Nora Baines said, "is our first text. There will be no one single textbook for the course. Now, on the supplementary reading list, the first title—which will be read along with de Tocqueville —is Mark Twain's *The Adventures of Huckleberry Finn.* I want you to think about the state of individual liberties in America as shown in this story about a boy and a runaway slave going down the Mississippi on a raft some twenty years after the Frenchman came here. Then, through historians and other novelists, we shall proceed more chronologically through the nineteenth century—but always keeping de Tocqueville and Mark Twain in mind."

"That supplementary reading list," Luke asked. "Do we have to read *all* the books on it?"

"Only those that are starred," Nora Baines said. "Like *Huckleberry Finn*. First two chapters by next class. It will do you no harm to read the other books, however."

"You mean, it won't do our grades any harm?" Luke said archly.

"That is also a possibility, Mr. Hagstrom. Not a certainty, but a possibility. As for those unstarred books, there aren't enough for everyone in the class, so you can sign up for the copies we do have with Miss Fitzgerald in the library. She's taken Mrs. Salters's place."

"Why did Mrs. Salters leave?" Kate seized the opening.

"I believe," Nora Baines said with unaccustomed hesitation, "she was offered a better job in another state."

"That's not what I heard," Kate said.

"What *did* you hear?" Nora Baines looked at her with considerable interest.

Kate tugged at her hair. "Just enough to know she didn't like it here anymore."

"Any questions on the assignments?" The teacher looked around the room.

"Has Mrs. Salters left for that other job yet?" Barney asked.

"Uh, no."

"Then I'll call her," Barney said. "Why she left might be a story for the paper."

"Well"—Nora Baines picked up her books—"that would be up to Mrs. Salters, wouldn't it?"

III

The next day Scott Berman, ambling down the corridor, just beginning to taste the after-school pizza only two hours away, felt a sharp tap on his shoulder. He stopped, turned, and saw an angry Gordon McLean.

"You read the first assignment in *Huckleberry Finn*?" McLean asked hoarsely.

"Naw. I'll do it tonight. It's not due until tomorrow. I never do anything early. Suppose the school burns down a week before the assignment's due and you've already done it. It's all wasted." Berman smiled, but McLean's scowl was unwavering.

"The book is full of 'niggers,' " McLean said. "Look."

He pulled the paperback out of his pocket.

"On page four: 'By and by they fetched the niggers in.'

"On page six: 'Miss Watson's big nigger, named Jim.'

"Page seven: 'And he got so he wouldn't hardly

notice the other niggers. Niggers would come miles to hear Jim tell about it, and he was more looked up to than any nigger in the country. Strange niggers would stand with their mouths open and look him all over. . . . Niggers is always talking about witches in the dark by the kitchen fire.' "

Gordon McLean closed the book and shoved it back in his pocket. "What the hell kind of racist book is that to have in a school. God damn! How'd *you* like to pick up a book you're supposed to be reading for class, and it's full of 'kikes.' On every page, 'kike' comes right up at you. How'd you like that?"

"Oh," Scott Berman said, "I'd just show it at home, and watch the fireworks when my father comes marching up here. That'd be the end of that book."

"That's just what I did." Gordon McLean nodded. "I brought that *Huckleberry Finn* home, and my father is calling Mr. Moore today for an *immediate* appointment. You know, I figured Miss Baines was a decent lady, but she doesn't give one damn about how somebody black like me feels having to read 'nigger,' 'nigger' all the time. And not in some Klan piece of garbage, but in a *school* book!"

"Unbelievable," Scott Berman said sympathetically.

That afternoon, in the coffee shop two blocks away from George Mason High School, Deirdre Fitzgerald leaned forward and asked, "What *did* happen last year that led Mrs. Salters to leave?"

"Well"—Nora Baines stirred the cream in her coffee

—"you've got to understand first that Karen Salters is no firebrand. The only crusade I ever knew her to get involved in was saving the whales. And since one of her ancestors was captain of a whaling ship out of New Bedford, I put that to guilt.

"So, when more than the usual number of would-be censors began to come around the school a couple of years ago," Baines went on, "Karen used to say, 'There aren't many books *I'd* go to the stake for.' She liked the job. She needed the money. What she didn't need was trouble. Her husband had been sick for a long time before he died, so that took care of whatever they'd saved. What I mean is, Karen wasn't carrying any banners. Not for the First Amendment, or anything else."

"What kinds of censors were coming around?" Deirdre asked.

"The standard brands. Parents who didn't want their children reading about sex or being exposed to words they weren't allowed to use at home. No problem there, of course, so long as they wanted to prevent only their own kids from reading those books. You'd just give the kid something else. But some of the parents wanted to save every single child in the school from those books.

"Then"—Nora Baines buttered her English muffin—"there were people who *said* they were complaining only for themselves and their own children. *But,* they'd pull out a list of wicked books that looked exactly like lists we'd seen from other folks who said they were only acting for themselves. I must say, however, some did come straight out and say they were part of an organization that was determined to clean up the whole school. And woe unto anybody who stood in their way. So it is that we have come to know, if not exactly love, Concerned Citizens, Parents for Morality in the Schools, and SOCASH. That is not a vegetable. That is 'Save Our Children from Atheist Secular Humanism.' "

"I think I know the answer to what I'm going to ask," Deirdre Fitzgerald said, "but which books were they after?"

"All the usual suspects." Nora Baines signaled for more coffee. "*Go Ask Alice*. Poor dead child. They think she's a vampire and keep driving silver stakes through her heart. And that aging menace, *Catcher in the Rye*. And, of course, sweet Judy Blume. With blazing eyes and flaring nostrils they have come after *Blubber* and *Forever* and *Then Again, Maybe I Won't* and *Are You There God? It's Me, Margaret*. Oh, my, I think they would exorcise Judy Blume if they could get her to hold still. And Kurt Vonnegut too. Although I think they would rather skin him alive—to see all the creatures from hell popping out."

Deirdre laughed. "Your review committee must be awfully busy."

"*That*"—Nora Baines banged her hand on the table— "is the problem. Oh, we have all the procedures ready to go. The complaint form for the child savers to fill out. The way in which the review committee is to be put together—from the school and the town—to examine the complaint. And if the book is arrested, how the trial is to be conducted."

"I don't understand," Deirdre said. "So what's the problem?"

"Our sneaky principal is the problem. Mr. Moore prefers to handle these complaints informally. They hardly ever get to the review committee. Mighty Mike meets with the indignant parent, or whoever, and then he takes care of the complaint."

"What do you mean?" Deirdre asked.

"Let's say it's a library book," Nora Baines said. "Not that we haven't had some complaints about classroom books. He handles those the same way. Of course, he hasn't had to deal with *me* yet. But if it's a library book, Mr. Moore would have a word with Mrs. Salters. She used to imitate his performances on those occasions."

Nora Baines squared her shoulders and, taking on a deep, buttery voice, impersonated Mr. Moore:

" 'My dear Mrs. Salters, with all the *good* literature available, surely we don't need the questionable books, the offensive books, on our shelves. This title, for example. A number of parents have dropped by to talk to me about it. Surely this one book is not crucial to the education of our young charges. I am certain, Mrs. Salters, that someone of your broad experience and knowledge will easily be able to substitute a more balanced—well, why should I be ashamed to say it?—a more healthy book.

" 'I'm not criticizing you for having ordered this title. Not at all. I am merely suggesting that if you will reflect on this matter with me, you will agree that this book will not be missed if it should be retired from the shelves. Or, if not wholly removed, at least placed on a restricted shelf.' "

"Oh, my God," Deirdre Fitzgerald said. "One of those."

"The Emperor of Smooth, my dear. Never, ever will you hear the word 'censorship' pass his plump, innocent lips. If Mighty Mike were a mortician, he would sooner give a discount than say 'death.' 'Passed away' is what he'd say. And so, when he kills or locks up a book, it is not censorship. It is simply selecting another book to take its place."

"And Mrs. Salters," the new librarian asked, "she went along with it without saying a word?"

"At first"—Nora Baines paused to finish her coffee— "Karen figured that one title, a few more titles, weren't worth a battle. And she knew there would have been a fight. A mean fight. Karen was no dummy. She knew, for all the honey on Mr. Moore's words, that she was getting orders; and if she didn't follow those orders, he'd make her life miserable. She'd seen what he'd done to people who crossed him.

"But after a while," Baines continued, "Karen got to where she couldn't stand figuring out what to say to kids who came in for one of those books and who had to be told it was no longer in the library or that it couldn't be touched unless the kid had a note from his parents. So I wasn't surprised when Karen, quite agitated, told me one day, 'This is not why I became a librarian—to keep books *from* people.' Soon after, she quit."

"Without a fight?" Deirdre Fitzgerald frowned.

"There was one," Baines said. "It was a doozy. But she's going to have to tell you about that. So far as the record shows, Karen left this school on excellent terms with the principal. She has a grand letter of recommendation from the book killer."

"Sounds like they must have struck some kind of bargain," Deirdre Fitzgerald said. "But what?"

Nora Baines laughed. "I am sworn to say no more. I've probably said too much already. But I did not want you to think that Karen was a wimp. She came through in the end. She came through beautifully."

Deirdre Fitzgerald put her fingers together and pressed hard. "And now . . . it's my turn, I suppose."

IV

"Gordon's pretty mad," Barney said as he, Luke, and Kate walked down the front steps that afternoon after their last class. "But he's missing the point. That's the way people talked then. Mark Twain is just showing the way it was."

"We all know the way it was," Kate said sharply. "That doesn't mean Gordon and the other black kids have to have 'nigger' shoved in their faces on every page."

"Some people are too damn sensitive," Luke said. "Nobody's calling *them* that. The book was written a long time ago."

"Just like a dumb Swede." Kate looked at him.

"Now that's different." Luke smiled. "You're making it personal. But I don't mind, honey."

"You watch that!" Kate glared at him and then suddenly smiled. "Okay, you're entitled. But I'll tell you guys something else. That's not all that's poisonous about *Huckleberry Finn*. I read the whole thing last night. All the women in it are yo-yos. You'll see. No, maybe you won't. In fact, I'm sure you won't. This book is just going to reinforce your ignorance about women."

Striding past them, Mr. Moore waved heartily.

"And don't you tell me"—Kate pointed to Barney as he waved back at the principal—"that's the way it was then. There were plenty of women in the nineteenth century who were strong and brilliant and talked back to stupid men. And who weren't always going around saying 'nigger,' like the women in that book."

"Are you saying," Barney said softly, "that we ought to take all the copies of *Huckleberry Finn* and make a bonfire out of them?"

"Crude. Sometimes you are very crude," Kate said. "What I am saying is that Mrs. Baines could have picked a book that isn't so offensive, that isn't so—so crude."

"Honey," Luke said, "you just did a great selling job. Now I can't wait to read that book. Nothing I like better than something that's real offensive. Keeps me awake."

"Do you find it's really worth all that effort?" Kate started to walk away. "Staying awake, I mean."

"Do you know what's the matter with her?" Luke said to Barney as they walked in the opposite direction. "She takes everything so damn seriously. She never has any fun."

"*That's* her fun," Barney said. "Sticking pins in people. And sometimes she has a good sharp point. But not this time. Still, I like her. She keeps *me* awake."

"Because she's so offensive?" Luke grinned.

"I wouldn't put it that way." Barney, turning around, watched Kate crossing the campus. "I wouldn't put it that way at all."

One wall of the principal's office was covered with framed photographs—all of them with himself, smiling, standing next to a visiting dignitary. There were at least half a dozen shots of Mr. Moore with the mayor of the town—a small, glowing man who had first been elected to that office before the students at George Mason High were born. Several governors were on the wall, along with judges who had also spoken at school assemblies. And there were a number of authors. You could tell they were authors because they were always giving Mr. Moore a book. Sometimes the book was upside down, but neither the principal nor the author seemed to mind.

There was even a Hollywood star on that wall. John Wayne. Years ago he had been making a movie in the town, and Mr. Moore had asked him to come talk to the students. Nobody seemed to remember much of what he had said, but everybody was very proud and pleased that Mr. Wayne had actually been inside George Mason High. Almost everybody. In the back of the hall, a few students—this was during the Vietnam War—

had been carrying signs asking John Wayne if he pre-
ferred his Vietnamese babies baked or fried.

A bunch of students and faculty members tore the
signs down and hustled the troublemakers outside. The
principal had apologized to Mr. Wayne. But Duke—that
was his nickname—standing up there so big and so
calm, he said he didn't mind those noisy students. That's
the American way, Duke said—speaking your mind
even if there's nothing in it. He got a big cheer for that.

Looking at the wall the morning that Mr. McLean
was due for his *Huckleberry Finn* appointment, it occurred to Mr. Moore that practically all the photographs
were of whites. There were a couple of black ministers;
the president of the local branch of the National Association for the Advancement of Colored People; a young
black soprano who had won a regional competition but
had then sunk like a stone; and a once and former
black member of the school board. But that was about it

Mr. Moore was wondering whether anyone in the
social studies department had a large photograph of
Martin Luther King, but he dropped the idea. It would
look phony—the only photograph on the wall without
himself in it. Maybe he could say he'd been sick that
day. No, too curious a coincidence. Well, he must invite
more black speakers. There was certainly an imbalance
on that wall. It would take a while to make it ten per-
cent black, but that was a sound goal. Mr. Moore felt
good at having made this affirmative-action decision.

He looked at his watch, frowned, and wished he had

made that decision some time ago. There was a knock at the door.

"Yes, Rena?" Mr. Moore said.

His secretary opened the door. "Mr. McLean to see you."

Carl McLean had done all of the talking, occasionally nodding to his son, first to supply a page reference, and then *Huckleberry Finn* itself—from which Mr. McLean would then read in a firm, angry voice. At least, the principal was thinking, the black parent had not seemed to pay any particular attention to the wall of photographs.

"It is not only the profusion, the infestation of the word 'nigger' in this book," Carl McLean continued. "I have shown you more than enough of that. Every time a black child sees that word, it is an insult, a profound insult. But underneath all these insults, of course, is the utterly barbarous attitude toward black people this epithet reflects. Gordon, that dialogue about the accident on the steamboat—"

"Page one ninety-three, Dad." Gordon handed his father the copy of *Huckleberry Finn*."

"They are talking about an accident"—Carl McLean looked at the principal, who was raptly following his every word—"and there is this dialogue:

" 'We blowed out a cylinder head.'

" 'Good gracious! Anybody hurt?'

" 'No'm. Killed a nigger.'

" 'Well, it's lucky; because sometimes people do get hurt.' "

The father closed the book and gave it back to his son. "Now," Carl McLean said, "there is no question that's the way most whites felt about blacks at the time. And if the truth be told, at the present time as well. But is that suitable material for a classroom where the young are presumably being educated to become, at long last, civilized in matters of race?"

"Well"—Mr. Moore cleared his throat—"it's been a long time since I read *Huckleberry Finn* myself. I guess I was about Gordon's age"—he smiled at the student, who did not smile back—"when I had to read it for school too. I did refresh my recollection of it, to some extent, last night; and while I am no scholar in the American novel, the possibility occurs to me that Mark Twain was expressing disapproval of racial bigotry in that passage."

Leaning forward, Carl McLean pointed at the book in his son's lap and then at the principal. "On that page there is not a line, not a word, of disapproval of the concept that black people are not human. Not from any of the characters. Not from the narrator, Finn. And nowhere else in the book is there any disapproval of the use of the word 'nigger' or of the diseased state of mind of those who use that word."

"But surely," Mr. Moore said soothingly, "in class discussion, Ms. Baines, an excellent teacher, and certainly a person without a speck of prejudice—"

"Now listen—" Carl McLean put a finger on the principal's desk. "I have no doubt that the teacher will say the right thing about how badly those white folks treated blacks. But let me tell you something, sir. What is going to stay in the minds of these kids, white and black, is: 'nigger,' 'nigger,' 'nigger.' And they are also going to remember the ignorance and superstition of the so-called sympathetic black character, 'Nigger Jim,' as well as the ignorance and superstition of every other black, without exception, in this book."

Gordon McLean was nodding vigorously at every point made by his father, who continued: "Mr. Twain was one hell of a good writer. That's why this book is still alive. So it doesn't much matter what a teacher says about it, how she explains it. The book speaks very powerfully for itself. And what it keeps saying is 'nigger.' "

Carl McLean rose. "Let me lay it right on the line, Mr. Moore. I do not want my son, or any other black child, to have to hear in a classroom, day after day, 'nigger,' 'nigger,' 'nigger.' It's demeaning and degrading and, if you will excuse me, *stupid* on the part of whoever selected that book. I believe I have made myself clear, and I expect the book will be pulled out of the course. Immediately!"

The principal also rose. "I hear you," he said. "I hear you loud and clear, Mr. McLean. And certainly, any parent who feels that strongly that a particular book is not right for his child—"

"Come on, Mr. Moore. I know what you're going to say, but *I* said *any* black child. Not just Gordon. No, that won't work—excusing only my son from having to read the book. It wouldn't be fair, in any case, because that book is a basic part of the course. If Gordon doesn't read it, he's going to know only part of what everybody else is studying. And on the other hand, for God's sake, they'll be talking about that book in class. What is Gordon supposed to do—hold his hands over his ears? There is only one thing you can do, Mr. Moore. *Huckleberry Finn* has to be *eliminated*!"

Carl McLean waved a finger at the principal. "And it has to be eliminated not only from the curriculum. That book cannot be allowed to remain in the school library for any child who may come upon it. You yourself said that your teacher would interpret the book correctly, and I pointed out that no amount of interpretation can undo the harm of that book's language. But for the sake of argument, suppose you have a point. All the more reason to remove the book from the *library*, where a child just picks it up, reads it—figuring it's okay because it's in the school—and gets no interpretation from anybody. That way the book is guaranteed to do harm. *Huckleberry Finn* has no proper place *anywhere* in George Mason High School."

"Mr. McLean," said the principal, "I very much appreciate your coming in this morning. We want to know, we need to know, our parents' concerns about the school. After all, you are our employers. On this particular matter, you will appreciate that I have to consult with the faculty and librarian, but I can assure you that this will all be done swiftly, and I shall be in touch with you very shortly."

"Give me a date," Carl McLean said.

"A week from today at the latest. You have my word."

"You understand"—McLean stared at him—"that I am not bargaining. Either the book goes, or there will be a mobilization of a good many parents besides myself."

Mr. Moore held out his hand. "Again, I hear you. It has been a pleasure meeting with you."

McLean just barely shook the principal's hand, motioned to his son to get up, and said at the door, jerking his thumb toward the wall of photographs, "Sure aren't many blacks up there. Maybe you ought to put up a group picture of the kitchen and custodial staff. That'd balance it out some."

V

The next morning, zooming down the corridor toward a class that had somehow started without him, Gordon McLean, seeing Nora Baines approaching, slowed just enough to proclaim, "Huck Finn is dead! *Dead! Dead!*" and sailed on.

"What on earth?" She looked after him, shook her head, and was about to go on when Maggie Crowley, a lanky, cheerful-looking woman in her late twenties, came around the corner.

Normally Baines kept her distance from Maggie Crowley, being suspicious of anyone in constant good spirits, particularly anyone teaching at George Mason High School. "You've got to be deaf, dumb, and blind, or loony," Baines had told Deirdre Fitzgerald, "to walk around like she does with a smile all the time." However, Baines had recently acquired a certain respect for Crowley. Maggie had not only created a new course,

American Problems, for this new school year, but had actually gotten the principal to approve it despite the controversies its guest speakers might stir up.

Crowley had worked on Mr. Moore all last spring; and he had finally given her a go-ahead only after having exacted a pledge that, as the principal put it, "Every single controversial subject—which means everything you will be covering in this course—must be dealt with objectively. It is your responsibility to see that *all* sides are fairly presented."

"How did you get him to even consider going for it?" Nora Baines had asked last May when the approval came through.

"Mighty Mike came to realize, with a lot of nudging from me"—Maggie had laughed—"that through the guest speakers, this would be a way to appease those parents who keep complaining that their kids only get the 'liberal' point of view on everything. From the textbooks and the teachers, and what not.

"There's some truth to that, you know," Maggie had said. "Nobody at George Mason teaches that the earth is flat or that the poor should all be sterilized or that the only way to deal with Russia is to cremate it. Though, from what I hear in the teachers' lounge, some of our colleagues do believe in one or more of the above. They just don't teach it.

"Anyway," Maggie had continued, "Moore likes being able to tell certain parents that, through my new course, the kids will be getting points of view at George Mason that they'd get in very, very few other schools.

Damn right. Like this whole shooting match was created in six days, and the theory of evolution is just monkey business. Hey, do you know that one of the anti-gun-control guests I've been trying to line up won't come unless he can bring his rifle? I said no, and he said I'm violating his constitutional rights. So I'm a reasonable person. Bring it unloaded, I said. But what if he gets accosted by a radical student? he said."

"Or by a middle-aged history teacher?" Nora Baines had sounded eager.

"Well, I told him that in this saloon, everybody has to check his guns at the door. The beauty part of this whole thing for me, Nora, is that the kids, by being able to listen to and argue with a whole spectrum of advocates—from Catholic nuclear pacifists to my gun-toting friend, and I'll get him—the kids may get the knack of thinking for *themselves*."

On this September morning, as Maggie Crowley came around the corner, she was even more animated than usual. "Hey," she said to Nora, "I'm having a debate next Thursday. 'Is Individual Freedom Getting Out of Hand?' You like that?"

Nora Baines looked uncertain. "Tell me more. Who's debating?"

"I've got a young lawyer from the American Civil Liberties Union and . . . I've got Matthew Griswold."

"Good Lord," Baines said, "the abominable founder and the chief executive officer of the Citizens' League for the Preservation of American Values. You think your young lawyer can handle him?"

"Well, if he can't"—Maggie Crowley smiled—"what about you? Actually, I wanted to invite you to bring your nineteenth-century American history class to the debate. It might be interesting for the kids to compare how the argument went then with how it's going now."

"Yeah." Nora nodded. "Not a bad idea. We accept, and we appreciate your invitation. Can my troops get into the question period?"

"Oh, sure. Just remember to tell them to leave their guns at the door."

That afternoon, Nora Baines's eyes were on Mr. Moore, who was standing in front of the wall of photographs in his office.

"I cannot believe what I am hearing," she said. "You are telling me that one of the landmarks of American literature is unsuitable for use in my class. Unsuitable for students in the third year of high school! I don't know why I said that. It would be just as outrageous to deny *Huckleberry Finn* to sophomores and freshmen and—"

"Calm thyself, Ms. Baines," the principal said softly. "The reason we have so much teacher burnout, and principal burnout, is that we overreact to every little frustration, and God knows there is no more frustrating job in the world than what we do. I have often said that I would have a longer life expectancy if I had spent all these years in the Oval Office rather than in this one."

He chuckled, but Nora Baines's face was of stone.

"Look," the principal said, "this is not a frivolous complaint. Nor is it a new one. *Huckleberry Finn* has been objected to by black parents and black organizations in other places. By respectable, responsible people, not extremists. It has been taken off high school required reading lists in Indianapolis and in New Trier High School in Winnetka, Illinois. You see, I've been doing some homework."

"I do not care"—Nora Baines banged her hand on the principal's desk—"*where* this book has been stomped on, mutilated, or burned by censors with the connivance—you hear me, connivance!—of people who call themselves educators. Who call themselves"—her voice rose sharply—"Americans!"

"Ms. Baines—"

"If you're going to call me anything, Mr. Moore, please call me *Miss*. That other thing sounds as if you were a yardman asking me if there were any more chores for you to do. Now, George Mason—the very George Mason whose name this school bears—said something you should know about. He said it in 1776. Note the date well! In drafting Virginia's Declaration of Rights, which led right to our Declaration of Independence, George Mason said: 'Freedom of the press is one of the great bulwarks of liberty and can never be restrained but by despotic governments.' And he did not mean just newspapers, Mr. Moore. He meant *books*, and anything else that comes off a press."

The principal moved to his desk and sat on its edge.

"This has nothing to do with freedom of the press, Miss Baines," he said. "We are not preventing anyone from publishing this book. However, freedom of the press does *not* mean that we must place in our school library, or use in our classrooms, every single book that is published. Freedom of the press does *not* mean that the First Amendment requires us to compel students to read a book that offends minority children and their parents."

"You know what I'm talking about!" Nora Baines struggled to keep control of herself. "You know damn well what I'm talking about. Freedom to publish is useless if people are not allowed to read what is published. And that certainly includes students. I still can't believe what I'm hearing. We're not talking about trash. We're not talking about a piece of pornography. We're talking about preventing our students from reading *Huckleberry Finn*! And why? Because it offends some people. Show me a book that offends no one, and I will show you a book that no one, in the whole history of the world, has ever willingly read. Mr. Moore, think of what you are asking of me! I am supposed to throw *Huckleberry Finn* out of my classroom! Have you no shame, sir? At long last, have you no shame?"

"Miss Baines," said the principal with a smile, "you are overwrought. Please believe me, I admire your fervor, your outspokenness. But I beseech you, Miss Baines, try to imagine yourself a black child, a black parent—"

"As if, as if"—she was breathing hard—"all blacks

think alike and act alike. As if all blacks are just dying to suppress books they don't like! Do you realize what you're saying? Talk about stereotypes! Oh, what's the use? I am *not* going to remove this book from my course just because you ask me to. We have a regular procedure, including a review committee, when there is a complaint about a book. I insist we follow that procedure."

"And you will abide by the result?"

"I cannot believe," Nora Baines said, "that a majority of any review committee will censor this book."

"But," Mr. Moore said gently, "if a majority *should* decide to recommend the book's removal from your course, you will abide by the result?"

Nora Baines sighed. "I would have no choice. I helped set up those procedures. But it won't happen." She looked at the principal. "Unless there's some funny business in the selection of the committee."

"As you know, Miss Baines," the principal said coolly, "the school board appoints the review committee. Are you saying the school board would engage in any funny business?"

"I am going to be watching. Very closely. If need be, Mr. Moore, the American Civil Liberties Union can be asked to come in on behalf of the First Amendment rights of the students—and of the faculty."

The principal smiled. "You say that as if I were Dracula and you were advancing on me with a cross in your hand. Miss Baines, I have no fear of the American

Civil Liberties Union. My responsibility is not to any outside organization. My responsibility is to the students and to the parents."

"You left out the faculty."

"Not by intention," Mr. Moore said smoothly. "We are all linked indivisibly in our common task. And that does lead me back to where we began this absorbing discussion. Since there is going to be a review procedure—though I had hoped to be able to resolve this complaint informally—the book, in all fairness to the complainants, will not be used in your course while it is being reviewed. If the committee does decide the book is appropriate, you can schedule *Huckleberry Finn* later in the year."

"No way," Nora Baines said. "This book is presumed innocent until proven guilty. That's what our review procedures say, Mr. Moore. Are you going to change them unilaterally?"

The principal rose. "The test of leadership, Miss Baines, is flexibility. Thoughtful flexibility—rather than rigid adherence to the letter of each rule and regulation. This school has suspension rules, for instance, but on occasion I have slightly reinterpreted those rules to avoid placing a permanent stain on a student's record. This has only happened under very special circumstances, of course. In fact, I recall your arguing very strenuously with me two years ago not to suspend a boy because of certain very special circumstances. And on reflection, rather than sticking slavishly to the rules, I agreed with you.

"Similarly, in the present instance, Miss Baines, what harm can it possibly do to be flexible, to show the black parents that we are sensitive to their concerns, and remove the book from your course until the review committee makes its decision? You didn't object to my bending the suspension rules just a bit? Why are you so rigid now?"

The history teacher stared at the principal, shaking her head. "You are incredible. You are the one who wants to suspend a book. That is the same as suspending the reason for all of us being in this school. Freedom of inquiry. Freedom of thought. Oh, God, why am I wasting my breath?"

"Are you saying, Miss Baines, that a book is more important than a child? That rules may be adjusted to particular circumstances when a child is concerned, but *never* when a book is concerned?"

With a sound that was somewhere between a word and a cry of anguish, Nora Baines stalked out of the room.

Mr. Moore, leaning back in his chair, was allowing himself a half smile, when she suddenly popped back in.

"I am *not* going to discontinue the use of *Huckleberry Finn* until the review procedure is *finished*. And if you try to force me to, I shall go public!"

"You already are," the principal said amiably. "This is a public school. Nothing is hidden here."

"You know what I mean, Mr. Moore. Not everything that happens here gets into the newspapers and on television. Yet."

The principal, his elbows on his chair, gazed speculatively at Nora Baines. "You know," he said, "a teacher who acquires a public reputation for creating controversy—even with the most noble motives—injures her credibility as an emotionally dependable, fair-minded guide to the young. I would be very distressed, Miss Baines, to see you undermine your fine reputation over these many years when, after all, this simply requires a brief period of self-restraint on your part until the democratic process at George Mason is allowed to—"

"NO!" Nora Baines, still at the door, shouted. "If this book is convicted, then, and only then—and with utter despair—will I stop teaching it. But not until then."

"I hear you, dear Miss Baines. I hear you. Take some hot milk before you retire, and we shall speak of this again."

This time she slammed the door.

And opened it again.

"I assume," Nora Baines said sharply, "that you have asked the parent to fill out a formal complaint form so that we can get this show on the road."

Mr. Moore suppressed a sigh. "I shall ask Mr. McLean this very afternoon to fill out the form. It somehow slipped my mind."

"Hah!" Nora Baines said.

"Anything else?"

"There'll be plenty else." She moved through the door.

"Gently, my dear Miss Baines. I've become quite attached to that door."

A few minutes later, the principal came out of his office, looked around the outer office to be sure Nora Baines had gone, and said to his secretary, "Rena, ask Miss Fitzgerald to come see me. Fit her in as early as you can tomorrow."

VI

Deirdre Fitzgerald was curious about Barney Roth. He was in the library so often, more than any other student actually, but he hardly ever spoke to her.

Looking at him going through the card catalog first thing the next morning, she thought: Either he never needs any help, or he's shy. Probably both. Or he resents me. Nora says he was a particular favorite of Karen Salters's. Well, I never did believe a librarian should force herself on anybody. Besides, I'm kind of shy myself, I guess.

But here he was, coming toward her. "Miss Fitzgerald, I'm looking for a book called *Banned Books/ 387 B.C. to 1978 A.D.* There's a reference to it in something I'm reading for Miss Crowley's course. You know, American Problems. There doesn't seem to be a card for it, though."

"There was a card," Deirdre said, "but no book to

go with the card. Somebody must have liked it so much he couldn't do without it. I have the book on order, but if you like, I have a copy at home you can borrow."

"Gee, thanks, I'll be very careful with it."

"Least I can do." She smiled. "You're my best customer."

"Where you worked before," Barney asked, "did you ever have any problems with people wanting to ban books?"

"Where I was before was in a private school for girls. The headmistress had a deep interest in the wishes of the parent body—in fact, that was her specialty as an educator. So she, and she alone, decided what books we would buy and what books we would not buy. Anything that might possibly offend any parent was not on the list. All banning of books, you see, was done before any book ever arrived. So, we never had any trouble once the books did come."

"Why did you leave?" Barney sat down on a chair to which she had waved him.

Deirdre laughed. "I think I just told you. I wasn't really a librarian there. Also, I wanted to work where there were all different kinds of students. A livelier place."

"I hope you haven't been disappointed," Barney said.

"Oh, no. You folks, as my father would say, are full of beans."

"Did you always want to be a librarian?" Barney asked.

"Just about always. I mean, where else can you be surrounded by friends who never die? I guess that sounds funny."

"No," Barney said, "not at all. If I didn't want to write books, I think I'd like to be a librarian or maybe own a secondhand bookstore where people could find books they've almost given up finding. My father spends a lot of time in secondhand bookstores, and I don't think he's ever left one of them without a bunch of books. My mother says he'll never read them all even if he lives to be a thousand, but he says that's not the point. He says, late one night, a book will come into his mind that he wants to read, and there it will be, just across the room."

"You must have quite a library at home," Deirdre said.

"Everywhere, the books are everywhere. American history's on top of one of the front hall closets. Jewish history is in Dad's closet. Hardly any room left for his clothes. Dad's an atheist, but he says there's a long, honorable tradition of Jewish atheism. He just tried to start a pile of Dickens in the kitchen. He said he thought Charles—Dad's like you, he thinks of all of them as friends—he thought Charles would enjoy being in the center of things. But my mother, she said that if he wanted Mr. Dickens in the kitchen, he could get Mr. McDonald to feed Mr. Dickens and everybody else in the house, because she wasn't about to duck books falling on her head with everything else she has to do. Don't get me wrong. My mother likes to read too, but she says books are a sickness with my father, and with me too. Anything you overdo, she says, is a sickness. Do you think so? I mean, about books."

"You know what my answer is going to be." Deirdre smiled. "Sure, you can overdo eating and you can overdo buying clothes or whatever, and you can overdo work, and you can overdo just about anything. But not books. Say, I was just looking you up. It's Barnaby. That's an interesting name. It comes from Barnabas, doesn't it? From the Hebrew, I think. Son of exhortation, or consolation? Do you know?"

"I should, I guess, but I don't. But that's not how I got the name anyway."

"What do you mean?" Deirdre looked at him quizzically.

Barney grinned. "I come out of a comic strip. There was this strip my mother loved when she was growing up. A kid named Barnaby and his fairy godfather, Mr. O'Malley, who had these magic powers, but somehow he always got it wrong. Things never came out the way he intended, not that he'd ever admit it. She kept a lot of the strips, and I still read them now and then. Anyway, Barnaby's parents never believed Mr. O'Malley even existed, but Barnaby sure did. He and Mr. O'Malley talked a lot, and they went out on adventures all the time. I think my mother really wanted to call me O'Malley, but she thought the kids would laugh at me. So she settled for Barnaby so I'd always remind her, I guess, of Mr. O'Malley. You see, even though he did make mistakes, Mr. O'Malley was a lot of fun."

"Well," the librarian said, "it must be nice to have

a name that comes out of so much pleasure. My name"
—her voice became low and deep—"comes out of
tragedy, terrible tragedy. Long, long ago, there was a
young girl, the daughter of a harpist at the court of an
Irish king. She was raised in seclusion because the king
wanted her for his wife. But there was a prophecy that
Deirdre's beauty—we're speaking of the past now—
would cause an awful, awful disaster. Not by *her* will,
for she was the most innocent of maidens. But prophecy
can curse even the innocent.

"Anyway," Deirdre went on, "she fell in love with a
young man, and he and his brothers kidnapped her,
spiriting her away to Scotland. In time, the old king,
the one who had wanted her for his wife, found them
and killed the young man and his brothers. In anguish
and in remorse—for she blamed her beauty for having
caused those deaths—Deirdre killed herself. There, you
see how lucky you are to have come out of a comic
strip?"

"I guess so," said Barnaby, "but Deirdre is a lovely
name. It sounds, well, like music."

"What kinds of books do you want to write,
Barnaby?"

"Oh, stories," he said. "Long, long stories. About
tragedy. And about funny things. About people I know.
Changed, of course. About people I'd like to know." He
smiled. "About me. I would like to imagine me in all
kinds of—"

"Deirdre"—Nora Baines strode into the library—
"we've got to talk. There's going to be one god damn

big explosion around here. Oh, hello, Barney. Deirdre, did you hear what our leader, our mighty leader, wants me to do?"

"Oh, my God," the librarian said. "I got a message to see him." She looked at her watch. "I'm late. I got started talking to Barney—"

"I'm sorry," Barney said.

"Oh, no." Deirdre smiled. "I enjoyed that talk a lot."

"Okay," he said, "so did I."

"I'll walk up with you," Nora Baines said to Deirdre. "I have to go to that debate, but I can fill you in on the way."

"See ya." Barney waved to them as they walked out of the library.

"Yes, indeed." Deirdre Fitzgerald waved back.

VII

Since the debate would be held before the two combined classes, and since neither Maggie Crowley nor Nora Baines presided over a large enough room, the event was scheduled for the auditorium on the main floor where John Wayne had once stood, as alive as you or me.

On the outside of the door to the auditorium was a sign:

IS INDIVIDUAL FREEDOM
GETTING OUT OF HAND?

MATTHEW GRISWOLD, CITIZENS' LEAGUE FOR
THE PRESERVATION OF AMERICAN VALUES
VS.
KENT DICKINSON, AMERICAN CIVIL LIBERTIES UNION

Luke shook his head as he read the sign.

"Out of hand?" he said to Barney. "This has got nothing to do with me. Not with the general I've got for a mother. I've got about as much freedom as if I were doing time. It's bad enough she has to know where I am all the time and whom I'm with, but she even opens my mail. Well, you know that."

"Yeah," Barney said, "but what I don't know is why you let her do that."

"What do you mean, why do I *let* her?" Luke said in exasperation. "What's my alternative? Turn her in to the postal authorities for tampering with the U.S. mail? How would that look on my college application? 'Mother: doing five to ten in the federal pen.' "

"I know what you mean," said Gordon McLean behind them. "My parents don't trust me for one second. They say I should be grateful I got parents who care that much about me. Well, you know, you can overdo caring. I feel like I'm wearing a collar. What about you?" He turned to Barney. "Your folks on top of you all the time?"

"No," Barney said, "not really. I mean, so long as my grades are okay and I don't come home walking sideways. Or upside down. They take an interest, you know, but they're not all over me."

"Barney, I'd like you to come home to dinner some night," Gordon said, "and tell my folks just that. Just that one thing. You got to be near the top of the class, you're the editor of the paper, and you never get into hassles with any of the teachers or anybody else. So you are a walking advertisement for the freedom way of life."

Meanwhile, seated behind a long table on the stage

of the auditorium, Matthew Griswold, who always arrived early for every appointment because that was a surefire way not to be late, was amusedly watching the lively interplay among the students as they took their seats. Including Luke Hagstrom's affectionate bouncing of a book off Kate Steven's head, and her taking the book and shoving it into his stomach.

A tall, bony man with stooped shoulders and sparse gray hair, Griswold bowed slightly as Maggie Crowley introduced him to Nora Baines.

"Are you going to be grading us on our loyalty to American values today," Nora asked with a wintry smile, "or will you just be debating?"

"Are you requesting a grade?" Griswold smiled.

"Only if I can test you in return." Nora's smile grew colder."

"On what?" Griswold persisted in being friendly.

"Oh, on *your* Americanism. On whether, for example, you agree with James Madison that the real danger to liberty in our democracy comes from the power of the majority."

Griswold looked appreciatively at Nora Baines. "That's too good a question," he said, "for a brief answer." He looked at his watch. "I wish *you* were debating me today."

His actual opponent, a short, stocky young man in his late twenties with light-brown hair and an armful of newspapers, from which a banana could just barely be seen peeking, rushed onstage.

"Sorry to be late," Kent Dickinson said. "The elevator in the courthouse got stuck."

"I thought the ACLU could work wonders," said Griswold.

"Hiya, Matt." Dickinson grinned. "If only the power of faith in the Constitution *were* that great."

"Ah, Kent," said the older man, "if you'd only put God on your board of directors, you'd never get stuck at all."

Maggie Crowley suggested it was time to get started. Dickinson was to be first. As he tossed his newspapers on the table, the banana slid out onto the stage and then onto the floor, to the snickering of the students. The young lawyer looked at it sadly. "That was my lunch. Oh, well," he said to the front row of students, "maybe one of you would hold it for me."

Going up to the microphone, Dickinson rummaged through his pockets, found a battered paperback, opened it to a page marked by a rubber band, looked up, and said:

"There was a man, a great American, who served on the United States Supreme Court for a long time. His name was Hugo Black, and he once said"—Dickinson looked at the book—"that since the earliest days of human history, I quote, 'Philosophers have dreamed of a country where the mind and spirit of man would be free; where there would be no limits to inquiry; where men would be free—"

"And women!" Kate shouted.

"Sure." Dickinson, startled, looked up. "Who said no? Where *all* would be free, okay, '*to challenge the most deeply rooted beliefs and principles.*' " He turned and looked at Griswold, who smiled and raised his eyebrows.

"Well"—Dickinson faced the audience again—"at last, at long last, such a country actually came into being. And you're in it. You're part of it. For the first time in the history of the world, here was a nation with —and I quote—'no legal restrictions of any kind upon the subjects people could investigate, discuss, and *deny*.' You've got to realize"—Dickinson looked at the students—"this had never happened before. There had never been a place like America."

He began to pour out some water without looking at the glass, and there was now a small puddle under the table.

"And then"—Dickinson tried again and half filled the glass—"Justice Black went on to say that the people who wrote our Constitution—among them, George Mason—knew that having a country with all this freedom going on could be very risky. With everybody constantly doubting and questioning anything they wanted to. Good Lord—sorry, Matt"—he nodded to Griswold —"you could have another revolution with all that freedom. So why did they take that chance? *Because* the one thing they knew for sure was that freedom, real freedom, is always—*always*—the deadliest enemy of tyranny. George Mason believed that, and Jefferson, and Madison."

He grabbed for his book, which was sliding down the stand. "One more thing from Justice Black. He was talking about the people I just mentioned, and all the other American revolutionaries who defied King George and the British troops so that they could live in liberty. But again, immediate liberty wasn't the only thing on their minds. They were convinced that, with all the risks involved, liberty would bring extraordinary advantages to Americans to come." Dickinson looked down and read:

"They believed that 'the ultimate happiness and security of a nation lies in its ability' "—his voice grew louder and louder—" 'to explore, to grow, and ceaselessly to adapt itself to new knowledge, born of inquiry, FREE FROM ANY GOVERNMENTAL CONTROL OVER THE MIND AND SPIRIT OF MAN.' "

Dickinson paused to mild applause from most of the students, although Barney and Luke were clapping vigorously, as were the two faculty members.

"He's not being very objective," Nora Baines whispered to Maggie Crowley.

"Maybe not, but he's sure being patriotic." Crowley laughed.

"Now"—Dickinson threw his paperback on the table. It just missed his water glass, to his surprise and pleasure. "Now, there are a lot of groups going around the country these days trying to destroy that vision— that marvelous vision of a country where individual liberty is so natural a right that it is in the very air the citizens breathe. I shouldn't say 'vision' because, with constant struggle, we've made it real. We *are* free. But if these groups *succeed*, liberty will be only a vision again—just the stuff of dreams.

"What groups am I talking about?" The young lawyer looked at some notes on the back of an envelope, and then stuffed it back in his pocket. "You can usually recognize them by how they call themselves. MORAL or MORALITY is in there somewhere. Or DECENCY. Or AMERICANISM. And each one of them has a list of things they want changed, you know; but what they really want is to have *everybody thinking the same way*. The way *they* think."

"Even if that were true," Matthew Griswold, from his chair behind the table, said mildly, "what's wrong with that? Isn't everybody free in this free country to try to persuade everybody else to his way of thinking?"

"Of course, Matt," Dickinson said heartily. "But the people I'm talking about are not content to see if their ideas can prevail in the free marketplace of ideas. They are trying to get GOVERNMENT to *enforce* their notions of morality, of decency, of Americanism. You see, they do indeed believe that individual freedoms are getting out of hand, that they must be controlled. But by whose standards? By *their* standards! And Government will be the policeman to make sure that everybody else falls in line with what these groups want."

Griswold was shaking his head while writing some notes.

"Let me give you some examples of what I mean," Dickinson said. "A number of these groups are getting school boards to censor books. To throw them right out of classrooms and out of school libraries. And in two cities—Drake, North Dakota, and Warsaw, Indiana— they actually BURNED those books. Like the Nazis did in Germany.

"And some of these people"—the lawyer took off his suit jacket and tossed it on the table next to the newspapers—"have been pushing hard to get the government to force prayers into public schools. But suppose you don't want to pray in school? Oh, they say, those students who don't want to, won't have to. They'll be excused from praying. But that way everybody will know who prayed and who didn't pray. That's not a choice anyone should have to make in public—in a school or anywhere else. You know why?"

"Because it's nobody else's damn business if you pray or not!" Luke yelled.

"You got it!" Dickinson smiled broadly. "Religion is personal, and it's a private matter for those who want it to be a private matter. Religion has nothing to do with Government, and Government must have nothing to do with religion. To make sure that in this country, everybody *would* be free to worship in his own way—would be free of any Government pressure to worship in the way the Government wanted him to—the Constitution set up what Thomas Jefferson called a wall of separation between church and state. And the Supreme Court has agreed with Tom Jefferson again and again."

The lawyer loosened his tie and began to walk up and down the stage. "But these decency groups and morality groups and Americanism groups, they want the Government to line you up at eight o'clock every morning so you can get ready to pray. Does that sound like a free country to you? It's *these* groups who are getting out of hand. If they keep getting stronger, what's to stop some Government official—somewhere down the line—from telling you not to wear anything red because that's the Communists' color?"

There were some giggles in the audience.

"Oh, you think it can't happen here?" Dickinson said. "Well, let me tell you something. In 1919 twenty-four state legislatures passed a law saying that if you hung a red flag out of the window, you were committing a criminal act. The next year, eight more state legislatures did the same thing. And so did some cities. Before that nonsense was all over, fourteen hundred Americans were arrested for breaking the Red Flag laws, and about three hundred of them wound up in prison. No Government craziness is impossible if people just let it happen. Freedom does not come with any guarantees, you know. You can lose it just by not paying any attention to those who are taking it away from you."

As he returned to his seat, there was more applause from the students. Dickinson got up, at first seeming to bow, but he was actually looking for his banana, which was suddenly tossed up to him by a student in the first row.

"I sure wouldn't want to be Matthew Griswold after that," Maggie Crowley said to Nora Baines.

"Don't engrave the winner's cup yet, Maggie. You haven't seen Griswold at work. I have."

VIII

Matthew Griswold, pushing his eyeglasses down onto his nose, walked slowly to the lectern. He opened a thin manila folder, glanced at it, and looked out into the audience.

"Let me begin with a story," Griswold said in a calm, clear voice that carried throughout the auditorium without any discernible effort on his part. "It's a true story. Not long ago, a brilliant neurobiologist from Australia was lecturing at Harvard on how the brain works. At the end of his series of lectures, he said that the theory of evolution certainly accounts for man's brain in its present physical state, but evolution cannot explain the mysteries of the mind. That is, the mysteries of thought, of imagination. Only something else, something beyond the capacity of science to explain, could account for these mysteries. This scientist did not actually say that these mysteries come from God, but some

of those in the audience thought that was what he meant.
And do you know what they did? They hissed him."

Griswold paused. "I told you this story not because
of that neurobiologist's notion about the limits of
science. I don't know enough about the brain, or about
evolution for that matter, to be able to tell whether he's
right or not about what he calls the mysteries of the
mind. I told you that story because my friend here, Mr.
Dickinson, makes so much of the individual's freedom
to *inquire*. Yet here was this audience at Harvard, presumably the very citadel of free inquiry in this nation,
and they could not *endure* listening to an idea that
contradicted their own religion—the religion of anti-
religion.

"Yet I would wager that every person in that audience considered himself or herself"—Griswold nodded
at Kate, who was not looking at him—"a true supporter
of individual freedom. That freedom to question, to
examine, that Mr. Dickinson described so beautifully,
so stirringly, as the essence of being an American. It *is*
a marvelous vision. But are those who hold it out to you
being honest about themselves? Do they really want you
to think for *yourself*? Or is it possible that they are as
rigid, as prejudiced, as intolerant as Mr. Dickinson says
groups with Morality and Decency and Americanism in
their titles are? Is it possible that while they sing you
songs of freedom, they are actually preparing you for
their own orthodoxy, their own standard tune to which
everybody must march?"

Kent Dickinson was looking at Griswold with puzzlement. Nora Baines was watching the tall, stooped man with reluctant admiration.

"My assignment in this debate"—Griswold looked around the audience—"is to persuade you that individual freedom has gotten out of hand. Well, my concern is not quite that. It goes deeper. I put it to you that freedom has become less and less *individual*. Instead of people who are distinctively, proudly individualistic, we are increasingly turning into herds. Can you imagine a herd of independent sheep? Let me be more specific. Let us focus on sex."

Matthew Griswold paused, correctly anticipating a certain quickening of attention in the auditorium. "If George Mason High School is like most other high schools in the country, some of you go to bed on occasion with others. Usually others of the opposite sex. On the part of the young women involved, despite the independence movement among women in recent years, how much of that sexual activity is really a matter of *individual* choice? Or is not a good deal of it coerced by the herd? By fear of being considered old-fashioned, narrow-minded, out-of-it, by your contemporaries? Is this individual freedom or is it just a new way of covering up traditional female subjugation?"

"What if a girl really wants to?" a male voice shouted from the back of the hall. "Would you approve of *that*?"

"No," Griswold said. "But I would have more respect for her if it really was a free choice. That it was not a better choice I would say was due to the failure of the school and of the young woman's parents to teach her self-restraint. To teach her that while part of each of us is animal, the more civilized among us do not eat off the floor or yield to every urge to copulate."

Groans, male and female, in the audience.

"Are those noises disapproval," Griswold asked, "or mating sounds? Anyway, I would rather this debate had been called: 'Is False Freedom Giving True Freedom a Bad Name?' Let me give you another example of what I mean. Mr. Dickinson listed among the enemies of individual liberty those who are trying to bring God back into the public schools. I am one of those. Does that make me a friend or an enemy of free choice? Think about it. Can you be free if you are ignorant of the choices you have? Imagine yourself back in kindergarten, and the teacher gives you a yellow crayon and a purple crayon. Just the two of them. And the teacher says, 'You may draw with whatever colors you like.' Is that freedom?"

Once more, Griswold paused. "This is a country," he went on, "in which there are no penalties for not believing in God, for not attending church. And I would not have it any other way. However, if someone who has spent his childhood and adolescence in the public schools decides that he is an agnostic or an atheist, is that really a *free* choice? Or is it similar to the child in kindergarten who has been given only two crayons? How can anyone intelligently, individually, reject God without ever really having had a chance to know Him?"

Dickinson was now writing furiously all along the edges of his newspaper.

"Mr. Dickinson, and people like him," Griswold continued, "accuse people like me of wanting to indoctrinate people like you, and he says that is why I am working to get God back into the schools. Has it ever occurred to you that you are *already* being indoctrinated, and have been since your first day in kindergarten? You are being indoctrinated with secularism. Godless secularism. How could it be any other way so long as there is a total absence of God in the public schools?"

"Why does God have to be in school?" Barney asked. "There are churches out there."

"Good question," Matthew Griswold said. "The answer is that school is just that—the place of learning. And no matter what happens or does not happen in your life outside this building, *here* is where you should be exposed to the most meaningful of man's accumulated experiences—and that includes faith as well as science. Otherwise your education is incomplete. Remember, I am not talking about conversion to or immersion in any particular faith. I am saying that at the very least, you have the right to experience prayer, which may or may not then take you to some particular faith."

"What if I prefer not to?" said Luke. "By saying I won't pray, why should I have to expose myself as an atheist if I don't want people to know what I think about religion?"

Griswold smiled with anticipation of his own answer. "Exactly the point made by my good friend Mr. Dickinson. If we had prayer in the schools again, the argument goes, those youngsters who would prefer not to pray would be too embarrassed to say so. Or if they did gather up their courage and leave the room, they'd be made fun of by their peers."

Holding the lectern with both hands and leaning into the microphone so that he could almost whisper and still be heard clearly, Griswold said:

"Are we speaking about America? A nation created and nurtured in dissent? A land where, as Mr. Dickinson told us so eloquently, everyone is free to challenge the most deeply rooted beliefs and principles? Are you saying, is Mr. Dickinson saying, that the best way to educate the young people of this country in our tradition of independence is to coddle them? To say: 'Oh, the poor dears are too soft, too weak, to stand up for what they believe in, and what they do *not* believe in.'

"Good gracious." Griswold stepped back from the microphone and raised his voice. "What a marvelous way I am offering for a youngster to learn that he can cope with being a minority of one or two or three if he chooses not to pray. What a marvelous way for him to learn how satisfying it is to *openly* fight for his principles rather than slink away. So I tell you, young man, that bringing God back to the schools may not only greatly illuminate the lives of many students, but it may well greatly strengthen the dissenting spirit of others, who will exercise their right to say *no* to prayer. And they will do so boldly, enjoying the feeling of being publicly courageous. You see, young man, nobody loses when God returns to the schools."

Maggie Crowley leaned over to Nora Baines and whispered, "I see what you mean. I never saw curve balls like that. Your head could come off trying to hit them."

"He's a cutey, all right," Nora Baines said. "I hear he may run for the school board."

"Lovely," Maggie Crowley said. "I always did want to be a cab driver."

"Let me answer another point made by Mr. Dickinson," Matthew Griswold was saying. "He tells us the Supreme Court agrees with both him and Thomas Jefferson, and not at all with me, that prayer can come into the schools without the Constitution crumbling into dust. Well, I would remind you that in the past the Supreme Court upheld slavery and then, after the Civil War, the Supreme Court upheld racial segregation. What I am saying, of course, is that the Supreme Court has sometimes been dreadfully wrong. And in time, it has recognized the error of its ways. So it will in regard to prayer in the schools. So long as the prayers are not of any *particular* religion and so long as no one is compelled to pray, God—as the Supreme Court will yet come to recognize—can lawfully coexist in our schools with Judy Blume."

"What *about* censorship?" someone on the edge of the auditorium asked. "Where are you on that?"

"I mentioned before"—Griswold stopped for a sip of water—"that there is no true freedom without a prior knowledge of choices. Now that should lead me to say that you ought to have access to *every* kind of book there is—no matter how trashy, pornographic, racist, anti-Semitic, anti-Catholic, antifamily, sexist.

"*But*"—he leaned forward again—"we must remember once more that *this* is a place of learning. And that means, for instance, that in order not to pollute your fine young minds with ignorance and superstition, your teachers do not tell you that the earth is flat or that two and two are nine or that Hitler was a terribly misunderstood man of enormous gentleness and compassion. No self-respecting school would teach any of that.

"Why, for another example, there are a number of books currently available that actually say there was no Holocaust, that there were no concentration camps, that no Jews were murdered by the Nazis. Under our Constitution, no one can stop such books from being printed or from being read. But *must* such books be taught in a public school? Is it unconstitutional for the school board to say, 'No, these lies about the Holocaust will not be taught here.' "

In the first row Gordon McLean was saying, "Yeah, but they're teaching some *other* lies here."

"Let me make one obvious point," Griswold said, "just so we'll all be clear what the issue is. Your teachers, your principal, are *responsible* for what goes into your heads—at least in this building. Once you're an adult, you can poison your mind any way you want to.

But so long as you are in this school, books must be selected for you. Or as Supreme Justice Hugo Black— one of Mr. Dickinson's heroes—has said, students have not yet reached the point of experience and wisdom that enables them to teach their elders. Therefore, in teaching *you,* your elders are expected to show *their* experience and wisdom. But occasionally some teacher or librarian does make a mistake and selects a book that will *mis*educate you, that may poison you. And when that happens, those mistakes must be corrected. By members of the community, if need be."

"Who appointed *you* the censor?" Luke asked.

Griswold laughed. "As a free American, I made a choice some time ago to do something about getting harmful books out of the schools, just as I would if you had rats in the basement of this school and nobody in charge here was doing anything to get rid of them. It is a citizen's privilege, and his responsibility, to pitch in and help when something's gone wrong with anything he supports with his taxes. That right is open to your parents and to anyone else in the community. We can all *appoint* ourselves, young man, and we should.

"But it doesn't stop there," Griswold went on. "Just as the President of the United States himself is accountable to everyone who votes, and just as the President can be kicked out if we don't like what he's doing, so it is with our very own school board. If they ignore my complaints about certain books that ought not to be in the schools, why, the next step is for me to try to get enough voters to agree with me so that we can change the school board in the next election. That's called democracy."

Nora Baines and Maggie Crowley exchanged meaningful glances.

"Wait a minute." Kent Dickinson rose from his seat at the table. "You haven't dropped the other shoe yet, Matt. You've said that there is no true freedom without knowing all the choices there are. Okay, but you've just told these students that they have no freedom to read what you don't want them to read. So you're limiting their knowledge of the choices they have. What happens to true freedom then? It seems to me there's a big hole in your logic."

"There's a hole in my logic"—Griswold smiled— "only if you're not used to thinking logically. It is one thing to say that students should know there is such a choice as religious faith—whether or not they elect to make that leap into faith themselves. But it is quite something else to say that students are entitled, as part of their formal education, to absorb, *under the authority of the school,* pornography, tributes to sexual promiscuity among adolescents, books that talk about kikes or niggers—"

"That's right!" Gordon McLean shouted.

"—or books that contain blasphemies against God, who cannot speak for Himself, in the school. If students want any of that filthy stuff, they can still buy it outside of school, God help them; but to permit anything and everything, no matter how false and vile, in the curriculum and in the school library, violates every sensible

definition of education. The students are here to become
part of the continuity of human learning, *civilized*
learning—not the diseased and vicious muck of man's
ignorance."

Mockingly, Kent Dickinson silently applauded
Griswold. "One thing that bothers me," Dickinson said,
"is that you and I might disagree about what's diseased
and what's healthy."

"Tell me, my friend"—Griswold turned toward
Dickinson—"would *you* allow a book saying the Holocaust never happened to be taught in this high school?"

"Damn right," said Dickinson. "You take one of
those books and you put it alongside the true record, and
not only will kids get a stronger hold on what really
happened by checking the lies against the grisly facts,
but they'll learn something else that's terribly important.
They'll learn the lengths to which anti-Semitism, or any
bigotry, will go to deny the undeniable. It's very useful
for young people to have some experience with that
kind of pathology."

"Well, sir," Griswold said, "you just give that little
lecture to the Jewish parents in this school if any teacher
or librarian is pathological enough to assign one of those
books."

"Your argument doesn't hold together, Matt."
Dickinson sat down again. "You don't help people
learn to be free by narrowing their choices."

"Freedom," Griswold said to Dickinson, as if he
were speaking to a slow pupil, "is indeed something
that has to be learned—unless we're talking about

chaos. And human beings become ready for different degrees of freedom at different ages. That is why we put the young of our species in schools. These students, here, even now, even though they are in high school, have not yet learned enough to be able to responsibly evaluate *all* the different pernicious choices in the kinds of books I say must be kept away from this school—as any carrier of infectious diseases must be kept away."

"So what you're saying is"—Dickinson looked up at Griswold—"God can come into the schools now, but later for a book in which a boy and a girl go to bed together."

Griswold smiled, "That is indeed what I am saying."

"How much later for pulling back the covers?"

"Oh," Griswold said, "if God comes first, they'll know when it's time to do that."

IX

While the debate was still going on downstairs, Mr. Moore, in his office, was taking a phone call from a member of the school board who had just been visited by a delegation of angry black parents.

Seated in front of the principal's desk, Deirdre Fitzgerald looked at the wall of photographs and imagined how she might brighten up the display. A Tenniel *Alice in Wonderland* drawing of the March Hare's Mad Tea Party with Alice, the Hatter, and Mr. Moore as the Dormouse being stuffed into the teapot. She giggled.

"Yes, I hear you, Mrs. Harmon." The principal looked somberly at Deirdre. "I understand how agitated they are. Yes, we certainly are going to review the book. At my request, Mr. McLean has just sent in the form that starts the procedure, and I shall appoint a review committee before the day is over. Yes, I shall keep you informed. Thank you so much for calling."

Mr. Moore put down the phone. "Well, Miss Fitzgerald, I trust you're settling in nicely."

"Yes, thank you," Deirdre said. And waited.

"Well, I expect you have heard something of the excitement about *Huckleberry Finn*."

"Yes."

"Miss Fitzgerald"—the principal leaned forward—"how many copies of the book do you have for general circulation?"

Deirdre paused and thought. "Let's see. The order for Nora Baines's class turned up somewhat short, so after I filled the rest of it from the copies we had, I think there are maybe two or three still downstairs."

"Miss Fitzgerald"—the principal smiled at her—"we don't want any more furor over this book than we already have, do we?"

"I don't quite understand."

"I think," Mr. Moore said slowly, "that for the time being, while all this is being worked out, it would be a good idea to collect whatever copies you have and put them under your desk. If anybody asks for them, they're out."

Slowly, firmly, Deirdre shook her head from side to side. "As I understand the situation, although the complaints have been specifically directed against *Huckleberry Finn* in Miss Baines's class, she is continuing to use it during the review procedure. That's the rule here, I'm told. So why should the book be removed from the library?"

Mr. Moore scratched his ear with irritation. "The complaint form I received this morning from a parent concerns the presence of the book in the *library* as well as in Miss Baines's class."

"Perhaps I didn't make myself clear, Mr. Moore," Deirdre said calmly, "but you haven't answered my question. I can't justify removing the book from my shelves while it's still being taught in nineteenth-century history. And it's properly in use in that class because according to this school's procedures, a book is presumed innocent until proven guilty."

"Well, well, well," the principal said sourly, "I know whom you've been talking to. Look—" A large smile suddenly appeared on his large face. "My concern, and I am sure it is your concern as well, is to minimize the tension, the divisiveness, the unpleasantness of this unfortunate situation. It would help me greatly if I were able to assure the black parents, while the review is going on, that as a gesture of good faith, we have taken steps to see that no black child will be offended by accidentally coming across the book in the school library."

Deirdre stared at him but said nothing.

"If it is decided, Miss Fitzgerald, that *Huckleberry Finn* does belong in our school, why, of course, you'll put it back on the shelves. What I am suggesting is just a gesture. A small extra step of understanding to show the black parents that we care about their feelings, their very strong feelings, on this matter."

"What about the very strong feelings of Nora Baines

and some of the rest of us who find this sort of side-door censorship exceedingly offensive?"

"Now, Miss Fitzgerald"—Moore dug viciously into his ear—"you're taking on an adversarial tone, and we are not adversaries. I have not known you long, to be sure, but I have known you long enough to be certain that you are not insensitive to the feelings of those who have experienced discrimination, cruel discrimination, throughout our history. Think of the kindness you will be doing them, with a small gesture of understanding."

"Oh, it's a bit more than that, Mr. Moore." Deirdre got up from her chair. "I did not become a librarian to hide books and to lie to children looking for those books. What you call a small gesture would be a huge act of betrayal. Self-betrayal, among other things. Shoving books under a desk! Really, Mr. Moore!"

The principal also rose. "You disappoint me, Miss Fitzgerald. Pride is a wonderful thing, but compassion touches many more souls."

"Is it compassion you're talking about, Mr. Moore, or are you trying to work things out so that you'll appear to be above the battle, no matter how it turns out?"

"How quick you are to be quick." The principal sat on the edge of his desk. "No matter how it turns out, Miss Fitzgerald, I will still be here, and I will still be dealing with these parents until their children are graduated. Even if these parents lose this battle, I want them to know they can come to me again because I showed real concern—since you don't like the word 'compassion'—on this occasion."

72 NAT HENTOFF

Deirdre shook her head. "But no concern, if I may say so, for the established review procedures of this school."

Mr. Moore, his hands heavy in his lap, looked at the librarian. "You are talking abstractions. I am talking about people. About black people who are deeply offended by this book."

"Mr. Moore"—Deirdre's eyes were large and angry—"are you saying I'm a racist?"

"My, my, so quick. So quick to miss the point. I am saying that sometimes a human being of whatever color is more important than a piece of paper."

"Including the First Amendment?" Deirdre snapped.

"Oh, well, you're a young woman, Miss Fitzgerald. To the young, there is only right and wrong, and nothing in between. I shall look forward to discussing these matters with you again in, oh, ten to fifteen years. Thank you for coming."

"Don't you understand"—Deirdre Fitzgerald was looking up at a defiant Kate standing in front of the librarian's desk a few hours later—"that there isn't a book in this whole library that isn't offensive to somebody?" Barney, seated at a nearby table, nodded in agreement.

"That's not true," Kate said. "How about Jane Austen's *Pride and Prejudice*?"

"No blacks in it," Deirdre said. "No Hispanics in it. No Orientals in it. How can minority students relate to a book in which there's no one they can identify with?

Therefore, *Pride and Prejudice* is profoundly offensive because it utterly ignores the life experiences of millions of people. Only a white racist teacher would assign—and only a white racist librarian would keep—that book."

"You're being deliberately silly," Kate said.

"Really?" Miss Fitzgerald smiled. "I've been at conferences where I've heard it seriously argued that even worse than books that stereotype blacks are books that ignore their existence entirely. And those books do not belong in a public school, whether they're literary classics or not. Kate, can't you see what I'm getting at?"

"No group should have veto power over what books we can read," Barney volunteered.

"Exactly." The librarian nodded her head. "Think, Kate. If *Huckleberry Finn* is going to be thrown out of school because it offends some black parents, what's to stop other groups of parents from getting up *their* lists of books they want out of here? Catholics, Jews, feminists, antifeminists, conservatives, liberals, Greeks, Turks, Armenians. Where does it end, Kate?"

"I don't play those games," Kate said coldly. "Those 'what if' games. All I know is that Gordon McLean has the right not to have 'nigger' shoved in his face in a classroom, and I have the right not to be forced to read a book that demeans women."

"But you and Gordon"—Barney was waving his hands—"can attack the book in class and show everybody else what you think is terrible about it."

"Why waste time on that sort of thing?" Kate said.

"We ought to use our time to read good books. I mean, positive books, books that tell the truth—and only the truth."

"Oh, my," Miss Fitzgerald said. "Oh, my."

"Well!" Nora Baines breezed into the library. "I have a copy of the complaint. Now at least we know what we're dealing with." She took several sheets of paper from a notebook she was carrying and laid them on Miss Fitzgerald's desk.

"Can we see?" Barney asked.

"Of course," Baines said. "This whole fight is about you folks and your tender, impressionable minds."

The form began:

CITIZEN'S REQUEST FOR
RECONSIDERATION OF INSTRUCTIONAL MATERIALS

Name of person making request: *Carl McLean.*

Telephone: *764-1987*

Address: *198 Cedar Drive, Alton.*

Complainant represents: *X* himself
                          X (name of
                              organization)
                              *the Black United
                              Front for Accuracy
                              in Instruction*

Name of school owning challenged material:
   George Mason High School

Title of Item: *The Adventures of Huckleberry
Finn*

Type of media (book, film, filmstrip, cassette, record, kit, other): *Book*

Author/Artist/Composer/Producer, etc.: *Mark Twain*

Publisher or Producer: *The American Classics Press (paperback)*

What do you believe are the theme and purpose of this item?
The perpetuation of racism through the stereotyping of Blacks as inferior to whites, and through the constant use of racial epithets aimed at emphasizing the inferiority of Blacks.

Is your objection to this material based upon your personal exposure to it, upon reports you have heard, or both?
It is based on my having read the book, all of it, and on my having been exposed to the racism it exemplifies from the day I was born.

Have you read/heard/seen the material in its entirety?
See above.

To what do you specifically object?
In addition to what I have already said, this book, even though it is allegedly sympathetic to the main Black character—who is introduced as Miss Watson's "big nigger, named Jim"—will reinforce the racial prejudice white students get with their mothers' milk. Simultaneously, this book will inflict pain and humiliation upon Black students.

What do you feel might be the result of a student's using this material?
See above. If you can see at all.

Is there anything good about this item?
Is there anything good about being bashed in the face?

For what specific population or age group do you believe this material would be appropriate?
Ku Klux Klan members over 70 to carry with them to their miserable graves.

Are you aware of the judgment regarding this book or material by literary or educational reviewers?
I don't need any "literary or educational reviewers" to tell me what's harmful, any more than I need nutritionists to tell me not to eat rotten meat.

What would you like your school to do about this item?
X   Do not assign it to your child.
X   Withdraw it from all students as well as your child.
—   Make it available only to those who wish to use it.
—   Other (specify).

In its place, what item of equal educational quality would you recommend of the same subject and format?
Of far superior educational quality would be <u>Great Slave Narratives</u>, selected and introduced by Arna Bontemps, Beacon Press, Boston, 1969. This is not fiction, but no novel could be as powerful as these truths, so long unknown to those who call themselves educated.

"Wow!" Barney exclaimed as he came to the end. "That's powerful stuff."

"I'd sure like to hear *you* debate Mr. McLean." Kate turned triumphantly to Deirdre Fitzgerald.

"I'm sure I shall have that opportunity," the librarian said. "I can't say I'm looking forward to it, but I'm not going to yield any more than he will."

"Right on," Nora Baines said. "Well, maybe I shouldn't be using that phrase in this particular context."

X

The head of the school board—he refused to refer to himself as the chair because he said he still had some mobility left—was Reuben Forster. His business, a chain of convenience stores that were open twenty-four hours a day, had been so efficiently organized by Mr. Forster that it practically ran itself by now.

Not that he didn't occasionally pay a surprise visit to one of his We-Have-It-All emporia at three in the morning to make sure it hadn't run out of beer or applesauce or light bulbs. But Mr. Forster spent most of his time on what he called his public business: the affairs of the school board; a senior-citizens center he kept supplied with conveniences from his stores; and, a special passion, a nonprofit summer camp for dogs. It was Mr. Forster's strong conviction that dogs need vacations too—especially from their masters.

A portly man whom no one could remember seeing without his pipe, Reuben Forster was much given to long conversations with himself when he had a problem to work out. Actually, the conversations, though he was alone, were with the people involved in the problem. He would assume their voices, as best he could, while asking them questions designed to make them more open to reason.

So it was this sunny morning, the day after the Griswold-Dickinson debate, in Reuben Forster's spacious office at the We-Have-It-All headquarters in the center of town. Puffing his pipe and walking slowly up and down the room, Mr. Forster turned to an empty chair in front of his desk and said, "Tell me, Mr. McLean, what if a white parent objected to a book written by a black author who preached that all white people are inferior?"

Taking on the clipped, swift voice of Carl McLean, Forster answered himself: "You have to name me the book and show me the specific passages where this inferiority of whites is preached. And then we will talk about it. But we are *now* dealing not with a hypothetical case but with a *real* book in *this* school. And in this real book, there are many passages that clearly preach the inferiority of blacks. That clearly say blacks are not fully human."

Forster frowned and said to himself, in his own voice, "What if we did have a book saying all whites are animals? Would I defend that book? Not if it was by some nut. But what if it was by somebody of historical importance?"

"You don't have to address that question now."

Forster's voice had become blunt and quick. "Because *Huckleberry Finn* is not what Mr. McLean says it is. It does not preach the inferiority of blacks. Quite the opposite."

"But Miss Baines," Forster said in his own voice, "that *word* is there. All through the book. I can't even bring myself to say that word, but good Lord, how can you expect a black child—" Forster shook his head and then went on. "I know your answer, Miss Baines. Mark Twain was *against* slavery. But that word, that word. Oh, my. I have another question. Should the meeting of the review committee be public?"

A deep, buttery voice now filled the room. "No, Mr. Forster. To make that meeting public would only increase and intensify the divisiveness over the issue. As principal of George Mason High School, I can tell you an open meeting will greatly inflame the situation. Let the committee meet by itself and then, when their recommendations come before the school board, it will be time enough for public debate. At least by then the review committee will have a clear, well-reasoned report on the matter, and that may bring some calm to the proceedings."

"I doubt it, Mr. Moore." Mr. Forster spoke to the air. "I doubt if we'll have any calm about this anywhere along the line for some time to come. No, it seems to me the more public participation, the better. Then there'll be no charges of a conspiracy by the review committee. Yes, that's what we'll do." He knocked the ashes out of his pipe. "Now, I'll have to meet with the school board and see whom we'll have on the review committee."

"*You* had better chair that review committee." A new voice was heard in the room. A high, piercing voice. "Everybody knows you're fair, so you're the one to chair it!" the voice continued.

"Why, thank you, my dear." Forster bowed to his imitation of his wife. "But I don't know that that's a good idea, because later I'll be chairing the meeting of the school board that accepts or rejects the review committee's recommendation."

"Nonsense," the piercing voice was heard again. "All you have to do when the review committee sits is to say you're not taking part in the decision at that point. You're just there to keep order since it's a public meeting on a highly controversial matter."

Reuben Forster filled his pipe. "All right, my dear. That makes sense."

"Mr Forster—" A squeaky male voice edged into the discussion. "We've had a lot of complaints about that new line of batteries. Customers say their being cheap don't do no good if they give out right away."

"You are at the wrong meeting, Oliver," Mr. Forster growled. "This is public business."

"I cannot believe this is happening," Luke, sprawling in a chair, said to Barney in the library two days after the Matthew Griswold-Kent Dickinson debate. Nearly everyone else in the school had gone home, but they, along with Nora Baines, were waiting to find out who

would be on the review committee for the trial of
Huckleberry Finn.

"I cannot believe it." Luke kept shaking his head.
"Just a couple of weeks ago, on television, I saw that
movie, *Fahrenheit 451*. You know, the one they made
out of Ray Bradbury's book. But that was in the future.
Way in the future."

"Where you been?" Barney said. "This has been
happening all over the country."

"Yeah"—Luke ran his hand through his hair—"but
it hasn't been happening to *me*. I mean, I heard some
things last year about some books just dropping out of
sight because Mighty Mike met with a parent or somebody, but I didn't pay it much mind. I should have, I
suppose, but I didn't. You didn't either." He pointed at
Barney.

"What do you want with me?" Barney frowned. "I
just became editor."

"But you were writing for the paper last year," Luke
said. "I don't remember reading anything about behind-
the-scenes censorship at good old George Mason. Or
was that because Mighty Mike wouldn't have let you
become editor if you'd made that kind of noise?"

"Damn it"—Barney glared at Luke—"you know
better than that. I tried to nail down a couple of those
stories last spring, but it was like catching smoke. Nobody would say anything. Mr. Moore would just give
me one of those fat smiles. Mrs. Salters said she didn't
know what I was talking about, and when I got to one
of the parents who'd supposedly complained, all she'd

say was she had nothing more to complain about. Anyway, good buddy, it seems to me we ought to concentrate on what's happening *now*."

"I cannot believe it," Luke said again. "Next thing you know those firemen from *Fahrenheit 451* will be coming in *here* putting the torch to"—he waved at the shelves around him—"all of this. And then each of us is going to have to memorize a book to keep it alive for generations to come. Man, that's hard work."

"Calm down," Barney said. "No way this review committee is going to throw out *Huckleberry Finn*. But it is good to have all this out in the open now—so we can fight it out in the open."

Miss Baines, who had been leafing through the *Daily Tribune*, snorted. "Barney, I want you to think about what you just said. Here we've got a book on public trial. No matter how that trial comes out, I think it's sad that it ever had to begin. You know, it's never the book that's really on trial. It's the author, even if he's dead. Remember that, Barney. Every time this sort of thing happens, it's a *person* who's being tried. For his ideas, his feelings, his memories, his fantasies, his yearnings, his language, which is his very self. To tell you the truth, I don't care *what* the book is. I hate to see words on trial. I get the willies. We're stuck with this trial, Barney, but we should not celebrate it, even if we win. Because putting a book on trial is wrong. It always has been, it always will be, and I am dreadfully afraid it will never stop."

Having never heard Nora Baines speak in quite this

way, Barney wasn't quite sure how to answer when a shout was heard, followed by Deirdre Fitzgerald's excited voice. "I've got it! I've got the list!"

Deirdre sat down at her desk and spread out a Xerox copy of the school board's appointments to the review committee in the case of *Huckleberry Finn*.

"You're on the list, of course?" Nora Baines said. "The librarian has to be on it."

"Well"—Deirdre smiled—"Mr. Moore said he was thinking seriously of recommending that the board disqualify me because I had already made up my mind. But I reminded him that our discussion had only been about his wanting to take the book off the library shelves *before* the poor thing had even heard the charges against it. I asked him if he was going to do the same thing to me." She laughed. "He backed down. With a very sour smile, I'll tell you."

"But you already have made up your mind," Barney said to the librarian.

She looked at him soberly. "Why, you know, Barney, that judges cannot come to any conclusion until all the evidence is in."

"The list!" Nora Baines said impatiently. "Who else is on the list!"

"I don't know some of these names," the librarian said. "Remember, I'm new here. Okay. From the staff, Helen Cook. Head of social studies department, right?"

"Yup." Baines nodded. "Very strong feminist. Thinks it essential that feminists make political alliances with blacks. One for the other side."

"Frank Sylvester. He's—"

"Chairman of the English department," Nora Baines said. "A straight arrow. Never uses any book in his own classes that anyone would object to, but he doesn't censor anybody else in the department. Says he's not a policeman. A vote for us. Maybe."

"Why maybe?" Luke asked.

"Because," said Nora, "I don't know how stiff a backbone Frank has when the heat gets put on him in public. Next."

"Two parents." Deirdre looked at the list. "Evelyn Kantrow and Stanley Lomax."

"Kantrow," Nora Baines said, "is a big wheel in the Republican party. Not only locally. She's a state committeewoman. Can't tell anything from that, though. In my experience, Democrats like to censor just as much as Republicans. Lomax is a professor of sociology at the college. And he's black. That's all I know about him. Except for his daughter. Eleanor Lomax is the most argumentative young woman I have ever had to teach. She drives me up the wall! But maybe that means they prize free speech at home. We'll see. Still, he *is* black. Mark Professor Lomax as a very possible vote against Huck."

"Are you stereotyping, Nora?" Deirdre looked at the history teacher.

"Move on" was Nora's answer.

"And two members from the community at large— Ben Maddox and Sandy Wicks."

"Maddox is an old party," Nora Baines noted. "A

lawyer. I don't know what kind of law he practices. All kinds, I guess. We're not a big enough town for specialists. Maddox has been around here forever. But I can't remember his ever having had anything to do with the school. Mark his vote unknown.

"On the other hand," Baines went on, "Sandy Wicks should be on our side. She's managing editor of the *Daily Tribune*. Good Lord, if journalists don't understand the First Amendment, who will?"

Deirdre looked up. "Sounds as if the committee could go either way. Oh, I found out something else. There's a second formal complaint. About sexism in the book."

"Ye gods!" said Baines. "Who's that from?"

"One of our own." Deirdre sighed. "A math teacher. Morgan, I think her name is."

"Oh, yes." Nora Baines sniffed. "Cynthia Morgan. Kate's in her class. A conspiracy, if you ask me. Just what are the charges?"

"All the women in the book," Deirdre said, "are caricatures. Sentimental, not very bright, sometimes just foolish. If they're married, they're subservient to their husbands. None of them shows any real independence. This kind of pervasive sexism in the book—the complaint goes on—is harmful to the self-image of every female student in the school and is also harmful to the male students because it encourages them to hold on to ignorant stereotypes of women."

"Humph!" Nora Baines scowled. "The women in *Huckleberry Finn* are no more foolish than the men in *Huckleberry Finn*. And the women don't go around cheating and murdering people like most of the men do."

"That's not all," Deirdre said. "Another complaint is on its way from Parents for Moral Schools."

"Let me guess what's bothering their pinched little souls," Nora snapped. "This book is unfit for school consumption because Huck and Jim were always naked on the raft when there was no one else around."

"How did you ever guess?" Deirdre smiled. "But that's just the first item in the complaint. Your friend, Huck, it goes on, is a liar and a thief. And he makes fun of religion and everything else respectable people hold dear. Also, considering that this book is being used in a *school*, Huck speaks very badly. His grammar is atrocious. Shall I go on?"

"A disgrace!" Nora Baines slapped her hand on the table. "This whole thing is a disgrace. But let me tell you something." Nora looked around at Barney and Luke. "This is going to be a very important learning experience. For all of us. Before it's over, we'll know who the sons and daughters of liberty are, and we'll know who the Tories are. Including the ones who'll be keeping their heads down so they can't be counted— so *they* think. But *I'll* count them, because you can't be in the middle in this kind of fight."

Deirdre, somewhat troubled, looked at Nora. "You sound like Madame Defarge. You sound absolutely vengeful, as if you're going to *do* something to every single person on the other side."

"I'm sure going to try, Deirdre," the history teacher said. "I have no more dangerous enemies than those who want to dictate what I can teach and what I can't teach. Who want to censor what *my* students can read and cannot read. Don't you understand that it's a matter of life and death? If I don't get these people first, sooner or later they're going to finish *me* off."

"You're right, Miss Baines," Luke said. "I can see those firemen, clear as hell, coming right into this library, and then going after books in every house in town."

"Oh, my," Deirdre said softly. "I do think we'll all be a lot more effective if we stay a lot more cool. And" —she turned to Nora Baines—"if we stay less personal. This is a *principle* we're fighting for. Turning everybody on the other side into a personal enemy really goes against that principle, Nora. They have a right to think as they do. They have a right to be wrong. Come on, next thing you'll be punching them out."

"The delightful vision has been in my thoughts." Nora smiled.

"Oh, great," said the librarian. "That'd help us no end."

"Don't worry about it." Baines laughed. "I'll stay cool, but I'll also be making up a list for later."

"I forgot something else." Deirdre looked into the manila file she had come in with. "There's something attached to the complaint from Parents for Moral Schools that fits right into your nineteenth-century

American history course, Nora." She found the Xerox copy of the sheet and read aloud:

"From the March 17, 1885 *Boston Transcript*: 'The Concord [Massachusetts] Public Library committee has decided to exclude Mark Twain's latest book from the library. One member of the committee says that, while he does not wish to call it immoral, he thinks it contains but little humor, and that of a very coarse type. He regards it as the veriest trash. The librarian and other members of the committee entertain similar views, characterizing it as rough, coarse, and inelegant, dealing with a series of experiences not elevating, the whole book being more suited to the slums than to intelligent, respectable people.' "

" 'The veriest trash,' " Nora Baines grumbled. " 'The veriest trash.' See how far we've come in all this time."

XI

In class the next morning, Nora Baines, pacing in front of her desk, was saying: "Now, Huck likes to be free, to be on his own, to just be floating down the Mississippi on the raft with Jim. Yet as much as he enjoys Jim's company, Huck often speaks of being lonely. Jim and the river aren't quite enough. Even though nearly every time Huck comes in contact with civilization, things turn out badly, he still needs, somehow, to be part of society. The question is whether someone like Huck *can* fit into society and, at the same time, stay as free as he has to be. And that brings us back to de Tocqueville—"

"I am not going to hear any more of this." Gordon McLean stood up. "I don't have to stay and be forced to hear about a book that insults me and everybody who looks like me."

"Gordon," Miss Baines said, "as you know, this book is now being reviewed to see if it should continue being part of this course. But until that decision is made, I am going to continue to teach it. You do not condemn a book, any more than you would a person, before there's a trial. If you would rather not be in class when we discuss *Huckleberry Finn*, I will assign you another book that the two of us will work on."

"No," Gordon McLean said. "I am not going to be part of this course at all until that book is gone. Gone without a trace." He looked around the room. "Well? Am I the only one who feels that way?"

Five of the other six black students rose and moved toward the door, as did three white students, including Kate.

"Hey," Barney turned around in his seat and called after the protesters, "for God's sake, this is a book about two people, one white and one black, who like each other a hell of a lot and who stick by each other. Is that what you're walking out on?"

"And the white guy always uses the word 'nigger' when he talks about the black guy," Gordon McLean said sarcastically from the door. "You know something, Barney Roth? You're one of those whites who talk a good game about being against prejudice and all that, but it's all talk. When the time comes to move, to *do* something, like walk out of this racist class, you just sit there. Talking. Talking. Well, I've heard enough talking. All my life, I've heard enough talking."

McLean and the eight other students left. Miss Baines rubbed her forehead, rubbed her chin, and looked at Steve Turney, a thin, bespectacled black student who remained.

"You want to know why I didn't go with them?" Turney said. "Simple. I haven't made up my mind yet. I'm the only person I allow to make up my mind. And I want to know some more about this *Huckleberry Finn* before I do make up my mind. So let's go ahead."

"This whole thing is about *us*," Kate would begin her speech whenever she descended on a group of students. As she did during lunch hour on the day of the walkout from Nora Baines's class. "So we ought to be there. We ought to tell that review committee we don't want a racist, sexist book in our classes. Monday night—in the auditorium. *Be* there."

Sometimes Gordon McLean was with her. Sometimes he recruited on his own.

"This is it," Gordon would say. "This is your time to be counted. Which side are you on? You still thinking like slave owners and slaves, or are you going to get this damn book kicked out of here?"

The other students, looking uncomfortable, just listened. Some said they'd be there Monday night, but few said which side they'd be on.

Meanwhile, the organizers of the *Keep Huck Finn Free* campaign were getting similar responses. There was a certain amount of interest in maybe going to see the review committee in action, but not much passion, one way or another, about whether Huck ought to stay at George Mason or go back on the raft with Jim.

"Well, look at it this way," Luke said to Barney as

they were walking across the campus. "I don't see a bonfire around here yet. We're that much ahead."

Barney shook his head gloomily. "What the hell's the matter with them? It's like talking to a bunch of sheep."

Kate was coming toward them.

"I hear you haven't been able to stir up the masses much either," Barney said to her.

"We've been doing all right," Kate said coolly as she stopped in front of Barney and Luke. "The ones on our side are solid. Solid like a rock."

"Another way of saying they're thick." Luke grinned.

"Tell your mentally underdeveloped friend"—Kate looked at Barney—"that I don't descend to that level of conversation."

"Kate," Barney said, lightly putting his hand on her arm and watching it dangle as she moved back, "if you win, where does this end? First this book. Then it'll be another book. It's like the Nazis."

"Barnaby Roth"—she pointed a finger up toward his forehead—"do you remember what that yo-yo from the ACLU said in the debate last week? That he'd allow a book in this school that said no Jews were killed by the Nazis, that there were no concentration camps, that the Holocaust never happened? Would *you* let that book in?"

"Sure." Barney nodded. "It's like the guy from the ACLU said. The best way to deal with lies is to expose them, to get them out into the light."

"The best way to deal with vicious lies, my friend," Kate said sharply, "is to not give them a chance to infect people. And that means killing them wherever you find them. Without debate. You can no more have a serious debate about whether the Holocaust ever happened than you can about whether blacks are inferior. Giving those so-called ideas the respectability of a debate helps them spread. So, if a book about the Holocaust being a fake ever came into this school, I would be leading the fight to keep it out, by any means necessary. And how a Jew, of all people, can feel differently, I don't understand. Unless"—Kate looked away from Barney—"you're one of those self-hating Jews."

"Hey"—Luke frowned—"I can see why you didn't want to descend to my level of conversation. You go so much lower."

Barney said nothing because he didn't trust his voice. He required firmness and anger from it, and he was afraid it would choke up instead.

That afternoon, Maggie Crowley, faculty adviser to the George Mason *Standard*, put the sheets of manuscript on the table, arranged them into a neat pile, and looked at Barney.

"What's the matter?" he said.

"Just one part of your editorial about Huck is the matter. The rest is fine, but I don't think you need this." She picked up one of the sheets and read:

" 'Can you imagine what would happen if George Mason himself was the principal, right now, of the school that bears his name? George Mason, the great friend of Thomas Jefferson and of free speech and press. *He* would be leading the battle for our right to read *Huckleberry Finn.*

" 'But what is the principal we do have doing? Nothing. He is not leading the fight for Huck and for us. He is not doing anything. He is just sitting back waiting for the verdict to come in. But if George Mason and his friends had not spoken out in 1776, this would be a British school today, and we would never have known independence. That's something for our principal to think about.' "

"The grammar's all right, isn't it?" Barney asked.

"Well," Maggie Crowley said, "it should be: 'If George Mason himself *were* the principal, right now.' But you know what I'm talking about. You are asking for trouble, Barney."

"I'm not going to ask Mr. Moore to write any letter of recommendation for me to any college."

"He may volunteer," Maggie said. "Mr. Moore does not like to be ridiculed. He most especially does not like to be ridiculed by one of his students. In public yet. And he does not forget such things."

"So what could he say"—Barney frowned—"if he wrote a letter about me? That I'm a good enough researcher to have found out that George Mason was against censorship?"

"He could say you are a chronically disrespectful, irresponsible young man who is always spoiling for a fight with anyone in authority." Maggie Crowley pushed her glasses down to her nose and proceeded. "His letter about you to colleges is also likely to say that if they admit this agitator—you—they will have nothing but trouble. And they will have only themselves to blame because they had been warned."

"Mr. Moore *would* do that, wouldn't he?" Barney sighed.

"He very well might. Do you really have to attack *him*? It's the book that's at stake. Mr. Moore is a secondary issue."

"No, he isn't," Barney muttered. "Miss Crowley, you're trying to talk me into selling out."

"That's crazy," Maggie Crowley said. "You won't be retreating an inch on censorship if you leave out just the part about Mr. Moore."

"If I do what you want, I'll be censoring *myself* about *him*, and I'll be doing it to benefit myself. That's selling out."

"Then you can say I'm selling out too." Maggie Crowley got up from her chair and walked to the window. "I am strongly advising you to cut out those two paragraphs for your own good—but also for my own good, and for the good of the paper. If your attack on him runs, Mr. Moore will be even more furious at me than at you because I didn't stop you. I mean, because I didn't persuade you to be a *responsible* editor, as he would put it."

"Responsible to whom?" Barney glowered.

"Oh, stop it! I'm not the enemy," Maggie Crowley said. "Look, I like doing this. I like working with kids —I beg your pardon, students—outside a classroom. Especially on the *Standard*. When I was in high school, one of my fantasies was being a star reporter, scooping everybody all over the world. This is as close as I'll get, and I'm good at this. I'm especially good at talking a lot of stuff past Mr. Moore. There are a lot of *those* sessions you don't even know about."

"I know about some that you didn't win," Barney said. "We've had to back down on some things."

"That's right." Maggie Crowley nodded. "But that's nothing compared to what's going to happen if I get booted out as adviser to the paper because I allowed this *personal* attack—and that's just the way Mr. Moore's going to take it—to go through. So which is preferable, my friend? Backing down once in a while so we can be free the rest of the time, or going too far in this editorial so that he'll send someone in to take over from me? Do you understand what I'm trying to tell you, Barney? In your way of putting it, I *have* sold out a little every once in a while in terms of the paper. But look at what I've saved. Look at what we *have* gotten in. If I stay—and I'm quite sure I won't if you print that attack—the paper will be a lot less free than if I don't stay. What would *you* do in my place?"

"I wouldn't have taken the job as faculty adviser in the first place," Barney said.

"But somebody has to do it."

"It wouldn't be me." Barney looked past her.

"So"—Maggie Crowley pushed her eyeglasses onto her hair again—"as a faculty member devoted to free expression, you would not be involved with the paper, leaving your hands absolutely clean, while the *Standard* was being censored week after week. Of what use to anyone would your purity be?"

"Okay, okay," Barney said. "Maybe if I was—were —you, I'd do what you're doing. And I suppose you're right that if those two paragraphs run, you won't be the adviser anymore, and that's going to be bad for the paper. But before I say what I'm going to do about those two paragraphs, I want it understood that if Mr. Moore *ordered* me not to print them, I'd get that ACLU lawyer and take Mr. Moore to court, and I'd win. Because this would be an absolutely clear case of prior restraint. The other times, he could argue we were being obscene or something like that. But this time, he'd be going smack against the First Amendment."

"You may be right," Maggie Crowley said softly. "You probably would win. But that wouldn't prevent him from appointing a new faculty adviser. Furthermore, the editor *next* year may be a lot different from *you*. He or she might be afraid to take Mr. Moore to court the next time. So, between the new editor and the new faculty adviser, where would the paper be?"

"I shouldn't rock the boat, right?" Barney looked at her.

"You shouldn't capsize the boat," Maggie Crowley said, "unless—"

"Unless what?"

"You will know, and I will know, when and if that time ever comes," Maggie Crowley said. "But as of now, where are we, Barney?"

Barney stared at the floor and bit his lip. "Without the two paragraphs, I guess. Well, I haven't deserted Huck Finn. It's not a complete sellout."

"Barney"—Maggie smiled—"you've got more courage than just about anybody else in this school, and I include the faculty."

"Thanks." Barney was not smiling. "So why don't I feel all that brave?"

"You want to run a picture of Mark Twain in that editorial?"

"No," Barney said, "I want to use a picture of Mr. Moore. You know, the one in the last yearbook. Where he looks like a real tough guy, like a general or something. And the caption will be: 'George Mason's principal leads the waiting for the censorship verdict on *Huckleberry Finn*.' Nothing wrong with that, right?"

Maggie Crowley laughed. "I wouldn't want to be your enemy, my friend. Oh, I almost forgot, you're leaving room for Gordon McLean's article on why *Huckleberry Finn* is not fit for this school?"

Barney scowled. "He told you about that? He doesn't trust me to run it?"

"I guess," Maggie Crowley said, "he wanted to make sure he was covered in case you got an attack of amnesia."

Barney scowled harder. "Gordon knows I wouldn't

kill his damn article. I'd look like an idiot, coming down against censorship while I'm doing it myself. But"—Barney suddenly smiled—"maybe he'll miss the deadline."

"No way," Maggie said. "He's in this all the way, just like you. And he believes all the right is on his side, just like you."

"Miss Crowley, how do you think it's going to come out?"

"I don't know, Barney," she said. "I really don't know. I wish it were over with. That much I know."

"But it sure is exciting. I can't remember being part of anything this exciting at school before. I mean, the First Amendment is something personal now, you know, not just some words in a book. It's *mine*."

"And what if they say it isn't?" Maggie Crowley asked.

"They'll be wrong, that's all. I'm not going to be here forever, thank God."

"But I may be," Maggie Crowley said.

XII

It was a little before 7:30 the next Monday evening, and Barney noted glumly that more parents than students were filing into the auditorium.

"I told you," Luke said, "they should have had a rock band to open this show."

Mr. Moore, who had been standing in front of the doors to the auditorium, came over. "I must commend you, Barney," he said, "on a very balanced presentation of this issue in the *Standard*. Between you and Gordon, all points were covered. I must say"—he chuckled—"I don't know why my picture was there, but I can't say I objected. Very nice shot."

"Yes, sir," Barney said. "Very rugged looking. Sort of like John Wayne."

"Well, I wouldn't go that far"—Mr. Moore smiled—"but I would not interfere with anyone's First Amendment right to say that." Laughing, he walked away.

"He never said a word about the caption," Luke said in mingled surprise and disappointment.

"Maybe nobody else will get it either." Barney looked gloomy. "Well, time for Huck's trial."

Kate, walking briskly toward them, slowed down briefly, nodded, and went on.

"She didn't mean what she said to me the other day," Barney said.

"I never said a word." Luke looked away.

On the stage, the seven members of the review committee were seated behind two tables pushed together. The chairman of the school board, Reuben Forster, holding his unlit pipe, sat in the center, between Deirdre Fitzgerald and Stanley Lomax, the professor of sociology.

Looking at the clock on the wall and then at his watch, Reuben Forster introduced himself and the members of the committee, bravely if poignantly announced there would be no smoking in the auditorium, and said:

"We shall be delighted to hear from whoever wishes to be heard. We would also appreciate your keeping your comments as brief as possible so that everyone who wants to *can* be heard. After taking testimony, as it were, the committee will decide if it is ready to vote tonight. Or if the committee feels more reflection is needed, it will set a date for the vote. I myself shall not vote, because the school board, as you know, must make the final decision, and I shall exercise my vote then. I do not believe in the doctrine of one man, two votes."

Mr. Forster waited for laughter. There being none, he proceeded. "I have a list of those who have already indicated a desire to speak, and then we shall open the floor."

For the first hour, the majority of the speakers were strongly, passionately critical of *Huckleberry Finn*. They differed only in what should be done with the boy. Some, led by Carl McLean, insisted that Huck be thrown out of George Mason High School. Period. Others, saying they were opposed to censorship, recommended that Huck be allowed to stay in the school but only under certain constraints. He was not to be made required reading in any course, but he could stay in the library provided he was kept on a restricted shelf, and provided that any student who wanted to take him out presented a note from home giving permission.

"Why torture Huck like this?" Luke shouted at one point. "Why not just take the poor boy out and shoot him?"

Reuben Forster pointed his pipe at Luke. "This is not a humorous affair, young man. If you can't say something constructive, stay silent."

"It is significant," a black father rose and said, "that this flip comment was made by a white student. Clearly, that young man is utterly insensitive to how black students feel when they hear classroom discussions of *Nigger* Jim and all the other *niggers* in the book. I ask you"—he pointed to the panel—"not to be insensitive to this psychic injury to our children. Let me put it as clearly and simply as I can. Why use a book that offends us when there are other books that can be used instead?"

On the other side, Kent Dickinson, the civil liberties lawyer, some parents, and a few students argued that Huck should not be deprived of his freedom. Dickinson, sometimes clutching his head as if to keep it from exploding, counted the ways in which the First Amendment—"the basis of every other liberty we have"—would be assaulted and gravely injured if this book were to be punished.

"There is the student's right under the First Amendment," said Dickinson, "to read and to discuss controversial thoughts and language. And the teachers' and the librarians' rights to academic freedom, which include the right to disseminate information. Also, there is the right of Mark Twain—posthumously, to be sure—to have *his* ideas, *his* language, remain free. Not just free inside the covers of a book that can't be opened. But free to be read and, of course, criticized. Isn't a school *the* place for free inquiry?" Kent Dickinson shouted. "Isn't this what education is all about?"

Kate, blazing, jumped up. "Yes, our freedoms must be protected. We have the right to be *free* of racism in our schools. We have a right to be *free* of sexism in our schools. And this book is both racist and sexist. Does the First Amendment really mean that schools should be free to warp the minds of their students *in the name of the First Amendment*?"

She glared at Kent Dickinson and went on: "Does the First Amendment mean that schools should be free to perpetuate racial bigotry through vicious, harmful stereotypes? If this is what the First Amendment really does mean, sir, then maybe it would be healthy for all of us to have a little less of it crammed down our throats."

"Hold on just a bit, young woman." The voice was deep and booming and came from Professor Stanley Lomax, a very thin and very tall man in his mid-forties. "If I hear you right, you're saying that we might be better off with a little less freedom to say and write terrible things about each other. Well, that's a mighty tempting notion. The one thing I don't quite understand, though, is who is going to decide exactly how much of our freedom it'll be good for us to lose."

"Well," Kate said, "in this case, you people on the review committee, of course. And the school board."

"Uh-huh." Lomax smiled at Kate. "And you trust us with this much power. But wait a minute. You don't know us. You don't know me, anyway. I've never had the pleasure of seeing you before this evening. Or do you trust us just because somebody appointed us to be sitting up here, and that must mean it's okay for us to have this kind of power—whether you know anything about us or not?"

"You're not just anybody," Kate said. "All of you were appointed by the school board. Why shouldn't I trust you?"

"Tell me, young woman"—Lomax was still smiling—"in this particular case, do you trust me more because I am black?"

"I trust you to understand more about the racism in this book," Kate said, "because you are black."

"Uh-huh. But let us suppose," Lomax continued, "that while I understand and condemn—that's what you meant by 'understand,' right?—the racism in this book, I am wholly insensitive to some other things. For instance, what if the book in question tonight were not *Huckleberry Finn?* What if it were a feminist book, and what if I were the worst kind of male chauvinist you can imagine? 'Keep the woman in the kitchen. Keep the woman pregnant. Anything else is un-American, and that's why this feminist book is un-American and should be kept out of this school.' Should I have the power to make that decision, or to be part of a group that makes that decision?"

Kate opened her mouth and then closed it. "Sir," she tried again, "if that ever happened, I would work to get you thrown off the review committee."

"Uh-huh," Lomax said and laughed. "But what if I had kept all that awful male chauvinism to myself, and nobody knew that about me. Except my wife, and she'd be too scared to tell anybody."

"Stop twisting that girl, Lomax!" Carl McLean shouted from his front-row seat. "This isn't some kind of game. This is about messing up the minds of children—including yours."

"Oh, I understand that." Lomax uncrossed his long legs underneath the table. "I'm just trying to figure out what some folks might be doing to the minds of children while *keeping* them from being messed up. The point I was trying to get to in my awkward way"—Lomax looked at Kate—"is that once you give people, any group of people, the power to censor books, you're opening up quite a can of worms. And sooner or later, they can turn on *you*."

Lomax shook his head from side to side. "That's a terrible figure of speech, isn't it? What I am trying to say, young woman, is that once you legitimize the power to censor, you can't be sure it's going to be the same people on that committee or on that board next year or three years from now. I mean, all of us here"— his wave encompassed the review-committee members to his left and to his right—"are wise, fair, compassionate folk. But we can be replaced by narrow-minded people who will arrest and convict books that you, young woman, would consider *essential* to the education of your classmates. In fact, from your point of view, your classmates' minds would be warped if they were *prevented* from reading those books.

"Now"—Lomax looked at Carl McLean—"when I was a boy in Georgia—1941, it was—there was a governor, Eugene Talmadge, who gave out an order one morning. All school libraries in the state, including college libraries, had to throw out every book—every single book—critical of the South, the Bible, and the state of Georgia. And that was one hell of a racist state at the time, I'll tell you. And still is, in a lot of places.

"Then," Lomax continued, "that good old governor

tried to get the legislature—this was two years later—
to burn, yes, I said *burn*, all library books advocating
interracial cooperation. He got disappointed in that one,
though. They wouldn't go that far."

"You're just rambling, Stanley," Carl McLean said.
"Let's stick to *this* book."

"Well, that's the problem, Carl," Lomax said amiably.
"It never is just one book, once you give out the power
to go after books. There's a school board downstate
kicked out *The Autobiography of Malcolm X* a couple
of months ago. How do you feel about that, Carl?"

"I'd take them to court if I were living there," Mc-
Lean said. "And I'd get that book back in. You can't
twist me, Stanley. One book at a time. One review
committee at a time. One school board at a time. Some
books I will fight for, and some books I will fight
against. You're talking absolutes, Professor. With your
carefully selected stories, you're saying no book should
be gotten rid of because then *all* books can be gotten
rid of. Well, if you'll forgive me, that is nonsense. We're
not sheep. We know what harms the minds of young
people, and we know what's good for young people."

"If I may break into this conversation," a large, blond
woman in her early forties said from the back of the
auditorium, "I would like to point out the *fundamental*
reason this book is unfit for our school, or for any
school. I shall read you one passage—and there are
many more such passages—that gets to the rotten,
morally corrupt core of the so-called hero of this book.

A boy whom Mr. Twain tries on every page to make attractive to young readers. Now, this is Huckleberry Finn speaking."

The woman, holding a paperback edition of the book, read:

" 'What's the use you learning to do right when it's troublesome to do right and ain't no trouble to do wrong, and the wages is just the same?' I was stuck. I couldn't answer that. So I reckoned I wouldn't bother no more about it, but after this always do whichever comes handiest at the time."

The blond woman closed the book and addressed the review committee: "Is this what should be taught in our schools? Is this what should be in our school libraries? The philosophy that since it's just too much trouble to do right, you just do what you please, you just do what comes handiest at the time?"

"If I may respond," Deirdre Fitzgerald said from the stage, "but I'm afraid I don't know your name—"

"Mrs. Nancy Dennis of Parents for Moral Schools," the blond woman said.

"Well, Mrs. Dennis," Deirdre said, "if I remember the passage correctly, it occurs just after two armed men in a boat—men searching for runaway slaves—are kept by Huck, through a trick, from going on board the raft and finding Jim. Having saved Jim from being taken, Huck wrestles with his conscience. In that place and at that time, white boys were brought up believing that turning over a runaway slave was the *right* thing to do. But Huck, by saving Jim, has just done the wrong thing, and he feels bad about that. But he knows he would have also felt bad if he'd let the men take Jim. So he figures: what *is* the use of learning to do right when you're going to feel bad either way?"

"And you think"—Mrs. Dennis reddened—"that's what children in school should learn—that it doesn't make any difference whether you learn right from wrong?"

"Oh, dear," the librarian said, "I guess I haven't made myself clear. Let me try again. Later in the book, Huck is torn again between right and wrong. He's sure he'll go to everlasting fire if he *doesn't* turn Jim in. But once more Huck does the wrong thing, according to what he's been taught all his life. He decides he cannot betray Jim. So you see, *that's* the right and wrong Huck is talking about in the passage that you read."

"I can read just as good as you can," Mrs. Dennis snapped, "and what I just read aloud is in this book, no matter how you try to twist it out of its real meaning. That book says it's hard to do right and it's easy to do wrong, so why not go the easy route? That's exactly what it says."

Deirdre sighed. "Have you read the whole book, Mrs. Dennis?"

"I certainly have, and I can show you other—"

"Do you remember"—Deirdre was practically pleading now—"oh, maybe a hundred pages after that passage you read, do you remember when Huck was trying to pray? But the words wouldn't come because he was not telling God the truth in his effort to cleanse himself of sin. The truth God wanted to hear, so Huck believed, was that Huck would finally tell Jim's owner where to find him. And Huck could not honestly tell God he would do that. At last, Huck gave up trying to be good, trying to be washed clean of sin, and he said, 'All right then, I'll *go* to hell.' He just could not let his friend Jim be taken back into slavery."

Deirdre stretched out her arms. "Don't you see? Don't you see what this book is saying? Your organization wants morality in the schools. Well, this is a very moral boy. Despite all the pressures on him to return Jim to slavery, Huck couldn't do it. He was too moral to do it. Don't you see?"

"The message of this book comes through very clearly," Mrs. Dennis said. "And that message is that a child ought to decide for himself what's right and what's wrong. I do not send my children to school to get that kind of teaching. I do not want them coming home and telling me they know better than I do what's right and what's wrong."

Deirdre sank back in her seat.

"I'm Mr. Dennis." A short, bald man stood up. "And I want to show you something else about this Huckleberry Finn and this Jim. This Jim, who always calls Huckleberry Finn 'honey.' "

Mr. Dennis took the paperback from his wife and said, "This Finn boy is describing here what it was like

on the raft with his friend Jim, a grown man. I quote:
'We was always naked day and night, whenever the
mosquitoes would let us.' "

Mr. Dennis looked around the auditorium triumphantly and repeated: " 'We was always naked day and
night.' " He threw the book to the floor. "No wrestling
about right or wrong there. I ask you"—Mr. Dennis
looked at Deirdre Fitzgerald—"would you—*if* you
have children—allow a boy of yours to be alone and
naked with a grown man who is also naked? What
morality does that teach our children?"

Deirdre roughly brushed the hair out of her eyes.
"Are you saying there is homosexuality in this book?
Could you show me, sir, one homosexual act in this
book?"

"Oh, come now." Mr. Dennis again turned to the
audience. "I'm not that stupid. In the nineteenth century, a novelist, no matter how perverted, would not
show such an act, but he could suggest what was going
on. What other way can you take that passage, madam?
'We was always naked day and night.' Huh? Huh?"

"What you are suggesting," Deirdre said coldly,
"never occurred to me. And I reread this book almost
every year. I suppose, sir, that shows you have a much
more richly developed imagination than I have. But I
do not envy you on that account. Not one bit."

"I must say"—Matthew Griswold of the Citizens'
League for the Preservation of American Values un-
folded his long, bony frame and stepped into the aisle—
"that while I certainly understand Mr. and Mrs.

Dennis's concerns about this book, I do find it difficult to share all of them. Young Huck, if you really look inside him, very much tries to be a moral being. Indeed, what has made him so attractive to young readers all these years is his need, his hunger, for justice. All through the book, Huck wants to be fair and he greatly wants adults to be fair, and he is grievously disappointed when they are not. On the other hand, he himself does lie, he does steal. But out of necessity, for Huck does meet some quite dangerous men, not the least of whom is his father. He has to trick them if he is, quite literally, to stay alive."

Deirdre Fitzgerald, puzzled, stared at Griswold.

"Taking the boy as a whole, however," Matthew Griswold went on, "Huck is not, to use an old-fashioned expression, a bad boy. For a youngster who does not go to church, except under duress, he spends a good deal of time thinking about good and evil. And as Miss Fitzgerald has said, Huck's greatest problem is that what the grown-ups around him hold up as virtuous behavior often seems to Huck to be hypocrisy and cruelty."

Griswold bowed slightly in the direction of Mr. Dennis. "No offense, sir, but I would say to you most respectfully that if the nakedness on the raft signifies anything, it further reveals why Huck lit out for the Indian territory at the end of the book. He could not stand, as he said, being civilized. That is, as he says at another point, he didn't go much on clothes nohow. Especially, I would think, on a hot night, out on the river. That's all it was, Mr. Dennis. I just can't bring myself to believe that Huck and Jim were, as they used to say, having an affair."

There was some laughter from the audience, but not from Mr. and Mrs. Dennis.

Having said all this, Matthew Griswold looked to the stage. "I nonetheless strongly recommend that *Huckleberry Finn* be placed under some restraints."

Deirdre, who had been smiling as Matthew Griswold talked of Huck's lack of enthusiasm for clothes, now watched him openmouthed.

"For all the values of this novel," Griswold said, "I am persuaded by my black friends that this book can do harm. I mean, of course, by its repeated use of an extremely offensive term that I cannot bring myself to utter."

Slowly, as he kept talking, Griswold moved toward the review committee. "Words are weapons. They can cause deep wounds, sometimes lasting wounds."

Carl McLean turned around in his seat and looked quizzically at the advancing Griswold.

"There are far too many wounds being inflicted on our black citizens every day." Griswold stopped close to the edge of the stage. "Why inflict more when it is not necessary? You see, the organization I represent—the Citizens' League for the Preservation of American Values—believes that a most fundamental American value is respect for each other. For example, I disagree with those who would try to keep God out of the public schools, but I respect them as individuals, and I hope they respect me."

Griswold looked directly at Carl McLean. "We need bridges, not walls, between us, my friends. As many bridges as we can build. And so, I hear and respect the deep concern and the deep anger of my black friends when they say that whatever the virtues of this, or any book, no book is worth the humiliation of their children."

Some of the students, black and white, applauded, as did many of the black parents.

"Therefore"—Griswold was now speaking to Reuben Forster—"those of us, conservative or liberal, who are not black but who would want our children to be protected from insult—from *school-approved* insult—should join these parents. As we would hope they would join us if *our* children were in danger of being humiliated by certain epithets in a *school* book!"

Deirdre Fitzgerald, eyes closed, was drumming her fingers on the table.

"I am not in favor of censoring this book," Griswold said. "But as I pointed out in this very auditorium not long ago, while adults are free to read anything they like—because they are responsible for themselves—young people are not—and cannot be—wholly responsible for themselves. And so far as their education is concerned, the school, *by law,* has the responsibility for determining what students shall read, and under what circumstances. And if the school fails that responsibility—not because a particular teacher or librarian is evil but rather is insensitive—why, then parents must intervene. As parents have here tonight."

"But you say you're not advocating *censorship* of the book," Evelyn Kantrow, a tall, brisk, gray-haired woman on the review com˙ ˙ ˙ ˙ ˙ ˙ ˙ ˙ "What *are* you advocating?"

"I propose"—Matthew Griswold's soothing voice bathed the auditorium—"that it be the decision of your committee to remove *Huckleberry Finn* from all *required* reading lists. That has already been suggested this evening. But I would not banish the book entirely from the curriculum. It is possible that certain students, under the direct guidance of a teacher, and with the permission of their parents, may be mature enough to benefit from the book as optional reading. My main concern is that it never be *forced* upon all students in a class."

Barney turned around to look at Nora Baines, whose face was grim.

"As for the library," Griswold continued, "I propose that it be the decision of the review committee that *Huckleberry Finn* is not appropriate for placement on the open shelves. But let it remain on a restricted shelf where a student may have access to it with the specific permission of both a teacher and the student's parent.

"It seems to me"—Matthew Griswold extended his arms as if to bring everyone in the auditorium into harmony—"that this solution avoids both censorship—

the book, after all, will still be in the school—and it avoids callousness toward the feelings of black students and their parents."

"THE HELL IT AVOIDS CENSORSHIP!" Nora Baines, roaring, strode down the aisle, stopped next to Griswold, and waving her forefinger under his nose, said: "You are keeping this book on the premises, but you are locking it up. House arrest is what it is. In doing that, sir, you are in deliberate contempt of my integrity as a teacher. Under your so-called solution, I am forbidden to assign this book to my students—no matter how strongly I believe, in my professional judgment, that it is important for their education that they read this book. You, sir, are handcuffing me as a teacher. The next thing I know, I shall have to present you, and Mr. and Mrs. Dennis, and God knows who else in this town, with a list of books for each of my courses before I am allowed to enter the classroom. PRESERVATION OF AMERICAN VALUES! Good God, sir, are you an agent of the Soviet Union?"

Griswold started to answer, but Reuben Forster, agitated, was banging his pipe on the table. "Miss Baines," Forster said, "you were not recognized. And it is not Mr. Griswold who will decide anything. The democratically elected school board makes the final decision, and that's as it should be in a democracy, so talk about the Soviet Union is way, way out of line."

"May I have a final word?" Matthew Griswold asked.

"No," Reuben Forster said. "I think we've had enough words for one night."

The school board chairman looked at his watch. "We have heard from all sides. Each member of the committee has, of course, read the book, but I am sure that each member is grateful for all the additional light—and heat—you have given us tonight. Is the committee ready for a vote?" Forster looked to his left and then to his right.

"I would suggest," said Professor Lomax, "that we sleep on it. I know I'd like to reflect on what I've heard."

The other members of the committee nodded, except for Ben Maddox, the elderly lawyer. Stout, with white, wavy hair, Maddox grumbled, "I don't have to do any more thinking. Couldn't be clearer. But if you folks need more time, nothing I can do about it."

"All right," Reuben Forster said, "the review committee will meet to vote within the next couple of days —soon as we synchronize our schedules—and you'll know the tally right away on the radio and the TV and in the paper."

"We want to know how *everybody* on the committee voted," Carl McLean shouted.

"Certainly," Mr. Forster said. "We wouldn't have it any other way."

"Because we are going to remember," McLean said, "how *each* member voted."

A few minutes later, with everyone headed toward the doors, Barney heard Ben Maddox saying to another elderly man, "Bunch of damn foolishness. Who the hell's more American than Mark Twain? So how can you kick him out of an American school? That woman was right. Must be a bunch of Communists behind all this. They're damn tricky."

"Well," Barney said to Luke as they went out the door, "that's two votes we got. His and Miss Fitzgerald's. All we need is two more."

"Don't forget that professor," Luke said. "The way he was going after Kate, he's got to be on our side."

Barney nodded. "We only need one more then."

Deirdre Fitzgerald, frowning, walked by.

"Looks good, huh?" Barney smiled at her.

"Oh, I don't know," she said in a low voice. "I'd feel a lot better if that Mr. Griswold had been somewhere else tonight. A lot better."

XIII

The review committee was to take a vote two days later in the conference room adjoining the principal's office; and that afternoon, waiting for the results in the library, were Barney, Luke, Nora Baines, and Maggie Crowley.

"It'd be great if we could win big," Barney said. "Something like five to two. Then the school board wouldn't dare turn it around."

Deirdre Fitzgerald appeared in the doorway. "No one won big," she said softly, "and *we* didn't win at all."

The vote had been four to three to adopt Matthew Griswold's proposal. *Huckleberry Finn* would be allowed to stay in the school, but under heavy restrictions. No one would be required to read the book for classwork in any course; Huck, subject to the approval of a parent and teacher, could be on certain optional reading lists; and in the library, he would be kept on a restricted shelf—available only with the written permission of a teacher and a parent.

Three members of the review committee—Deirdre, Professor Lomax, and Ben Maddox—had been in favor of letting Huck Finn roam freely throughout George Mason High School.

"You mean to tell me"—Nora Baines broke a pencil in two—"that if only one of our two faculty members on that committee had voted right, we would have won? What did those two creeps have to say for themselves?"

"Both Helen Cook and Frank Sylvester," Deirdre said, "thought it very important not to offend the black students and their parents; and under what they call the Griswold Compromise, they don't have to do that. Meanwhile, the book is not being censored because it's still in the school. As for Evelyn Kantrow—you know, the other parent besides Professor Lomax—she was very nervous about that boy and that man together, stark naked, on that raft. She told us she didn't remember all that nakedness being in the book, but she bought a copy yesterday and, by gum, there it was. Mr. Twain, she said, was a very sneaky, dirty-minded man, and she's now going to go through all his other books in the school."

"I know whose mind should be washed out with soap." Nora Baines sniffed. "But, Deirdre, what about Sandy Wicks? I was sure a journalist would be against censorship or whatever the hell Griswold and his comrades choose to call it."

Deirdre shook her head mournfully. "Wicks was with us until Griswold turned her around. He made it sound —to some folks, anyway—that if you didn't think the way he did, you were insensitive and cruel and probably a racist. And Sandy Wicks, good liberal that she is, does not want to think of herself as any one of those things. But she did tell me when it was all over that she would never have agreed to just throw the book out of the school."

"How noble of her," Maggie Crowley said. "Putting Huck in shackles on a back shelf, that's the liberal thing to do, right?"

"So what are *we* going to do?" Luke looked all around.

Deirdre Fitzgerald sat down on the edge of her desk. "The school board meeting at which this decision will be accepted or turned down is going to be two weeks from tonight. We've got to organize. We've got to spread the word so that a lot of *our* people—if we have a lot of people—will be at that meeting. Leaflets, letters to the editor of the *Daily Tribune*, and maybe we can scrape up enough money for an ad. And you"—Deirdre turned to Barney—"you'll be doing a story for the *Standard*, right? So maybe that'll get a lot more students to come."

Barney nodded. "And there may be an exclusive in that story."

Deirdre looked at him. "Like what?"

"Mrs. Salters said she'd see me," Barney said, "if the review committee voted the wrong way.

In Karen Salters's small, neat living room the next afternoon, Barney took a seat on the sofa and placed his notebook on the table in front of it.

A small, rather nervous woman, her brown hair drawn tightly back, Mrs. Salters looked so intently at Barney that *he* was becoming rather nervous.

"It took me quite a while to find a new job," she began. "I don't start until January. It's not in this state. And I certainly did not intend to get involved in a public controversy in the short time I have left in this town." She started to sit down in a chair opposite Barney but stopped. "I'm sorry, would you like a Coca-Cola or something?"

Barney declined.

Sitting straight-backed in the chair, the former librarian at the high school went on. "It's just that this is too much. Attacking *Huckleberry Finn*! Do you know what Lionel Trilling said about *Huckleberry Finn*?"

Barney, wondering who Lionel Trilling was, said he did not.

"Wait a minute." She left the living room, went upstairs, and returned with a paperback book. "Here it is. Here is what this extraordinarily perceptive literary critic, maybe the best we have ever had, says about this terribly harmful book that they want to keep locked up." Mrs. Salters opened the book.

" 'One can read it at ten and then annually ever after, and each year find that it is as fresh as the year before, that it has changed only in becoming somewhat larger. To read it young is like planting a tree young—each year adds a new growth ring of learning, and the book is as little likely as the tree to become dull. So we may imagine an Athenian boy grew up together with the *Odyssey*. There are few other books which we can know so young and love so long.' "

By the last sentence, Karen Salters's voice had started to tremble, and Barney, seeing tears in her eyes, looked away.

"Imagine," she said, closing the book, "depriving students of such a book. Well"—Mrs. Salters raised her head, her voice firm again—"I intend to do whatever I can to stop this nonsense. What is needed now, young man, is ridicule. The best weapon against fools is to make them look as foolish as they are. And the biggest fool—as well as the biggest coward in all of this—is Mr. Moore. He could have turned this all around if he had forcefully reminded people, especially the review committee, what a school is for. It's for opening the minds of the young—not locking up books. But *he* doesn't know what a school is for."

She got up from her chair and stood against the wall, looking steadily at Barney. "All right, young man, it is time to begin. During the two years before I left George Mason, there had been a growing number of what I shall call censorship incidents. A parent complaining about a book in the library, and the Emperor of Smooth —Mr. Moore—coming to me and telling me to take that book off the shelves. Well, I—I am not much of a fighter and, I am ashamed to tell you this, I went along. I like this town, I grew up in this town, I was graduated from George Mason, and I didn't want to lose my job there."

The church clock across the street was striking five. "A lovely, mournful sound," Mrs. Salters said. "I shall miss those bells. However. As these incidents continued, it was getting harder and harder for me to just follow orders. I felt like such a—a collaborator. A collaborator in evil. What's the difference between burning a book, like the Nazis did, and hiding it?

"Then one day, he came to me, that oleaginous man, and said that *Our Mutual Friend* would have to be taken off the open shelves. I must tell you, young man, that Charles Dickens is my oldest and most reliable friend. I have every one of his novels, and I keep coming back to them. It may be, it probably is, a deficiency in my character, but the people in Mr. Dickens's books are more real to me, more dear to me, than most of the people I know in so-called real life. So Mr. Moore was telling me to lock up a book by my best friend—a book that was full of real people I had known for so many years."

"What could there be in a Charles Dickens novel that would offend anyone?" Barney asked.

Karen Salters smiled thinly. "There are people who

are offended that everyone, in or out of books, is not exactly like them. But, to be specific, the parent who had complained about *Our Mutual Friend* objected, he said, to the violence in the book. There *is* murder, and attempted murder besides, although all the evildoers are ultimately punished. Quite dreadfully punished.

"The parent also complained," she went on, "that there is lust in the book. And so there is; but the person who lusted after a marvelously brave young woman never fulfilled his intentions. And as a consequence of his lust, he died a terrible death. The parent had one more complaint. There is anti-Semitism in the book, he charged. True. A despicable character *is* anti-Semitic, and one of the ways Dickens makes him so despicable is by showing this character's vicious bigotry. Oh, I can't go on defending a book that needs no defense."

Karen Salters left her place by the wall and seated herself opposite Barney. "Well, I told Mr. Moore— who, of course, had not read *Our Mutual Friend* but would have acted the same way if he had—I told him the very same things I have just told you. He would not be moved. A parent had complained, and *Our Mutual Friend* had to be put away. I brooded and brooded. I should have just quit, but, well, as I told you, I did so like being the librarian where I had gone to school. Are you sure you wouldn't like a Coca-Cola?"

Barney was sure.

"I sent Mr. Moore a letter," she continued. "I told him I had discovered an extremely troubling section in a book in the library, and I wanted his advice as to whether we should remove that book from the shelves before there were complaints. Because surely there would be a great fuss once a parent found out about those passages.

"The story"—Karen Salters looked as if she were still shocked by the memory of it—"was about a man, a family man, who also lived with a concubine. Do you know what that is?"

"A woman who stays with a man but she's not married to him," Barney answered.

"Quite right. How did they ever let you learn that? Anyway, in a fit of anger, this concubine left the man she had been living with and went back to her father's house many miles away. The man she had left went after her. He persuaded his concubine to return with him; and on the way back, as the sun was setting, they needed a place to stay for the night in a town that turned out to be unfriendly. But one person did take them in. While they were all having dinner, some awful, awful men in the neighborhood tried to break into the house because they wanted to have sex with the man who was traveling with his concubine."

Barney frowned. "With the man?"

"With the man," Karen Salters said firmly. "They wanted to rape the man. Well, he didn't want to be raped. So he took his concubine and offered her to these men. They took her and sexually abused her all through the night. At dawn they let her go, and when the man came out of the house the next morning to continue his journey home, he found his concubine on the threshold. She was dead. He put her body across his donkey, and when he got home, he took a knife and cut her into twelve pieces."

Barney looked decidedly uncomfortable. "What a sick story."

"He then sent those pieces of her body," Karen Salters continued calmly, "to the heads of the towns and cities in the land in which he lived. He asked them for help in taking vengeance against the men who had abused her and killed her. And she was avenged."

"Wow," Barney said, "*that* is a disgusting story. What awful kind of book is it in?"

Karen Salters smiled. "The book containing that story, young man, is the Bible. To be specific, it's in Chapter Nineteen of the Book of Judges."

"But"—Barney was puzzled—"why did you call Mr. Moore's attention to it then? You can't throw the Bible out of the library."

"Precisely my point," she said triumphantly. "Here was my old, dear friend, Charles Dickens, being punished for something so much milder, so much less shocking, than this story from the Bible. I told Mr. Moore that if he went ahead and locked up *Our Mutual Friend,* I would write to the newspapers and to the television stations and I would compare the passages from Mr. Dickens that the parent complained about with the story I just told you. And I would point out that Mr. Dickens was being treated very unfairly.

"Mr. Moore came to see me as soon as he received my letter, and, I must say, he was extremely angry.

How dare I try to embarrass him? If I were to go public on this matter, he would fire me, he said. But I told him that if he fired me, I would reveal all the books he had sneakily censored, in one way or another, during the past couple of years—without going through the school's review procedures. Why shouldn't I tell? What would I have to lose if I were fired?"

Karen Salters stopped and listened. But there were no sounds outside.

"Well," she went on, "Mr. Moore huffed and puffed for quite a while. Firing me had suddenly lost its attractiveness, but he also wanted to soothe the parent complaining about Mr. Dickens. Would you believe that at one point he was thinking about keeping both *Our Mutual Friend* and the Bible in a locked cabinet? That idea lasted about two seconds. Of course, he couldn't lock up the Bible. But then he decided that he *could* remove the nineteenth chapter of Judges from all the Bibles in the library. Nobody ever read in that part of the Bible, so nobody would notice the difference."

"He was going to tear pages out of the Bible?" Barney was incredulous.

"He did. He did vandalize one copy of the Bible. And it wasn't the first time he'd torn pages out of a book," Karen Salters said dryly. "I could name you several poetry anthologies in the library that are no longer quite whole. Anyway, I told Mr. Moore that even if he went on to tear those pages out of every Bible we had, he couldn't stop there. 'Read,' I said, 'the thirteenth chapter in the second Book of Samuel.' "

"What's in there?" Barney asked.

"One of King David's sons rapes his sister."

"Oh, my God."

"I said to Mr. Moore that it just wouldn't do. If he decided to rip out section after section of the Bible, he would be a laughingstock. Not only here but all over the country. I mean, you're a journalist, young man. Is there a newspaper that wouldn't love to get the story of a high school principal making the Bible fit for his students to read by stripping it of its lewd passages?"

"I guess not," Barney said. "Gee, I had no idea that sort of stuff was in the Bible."

"Your friend Mr. Twain did." Karen Salters walked over to a small desk in the living room, picked up a slip of paper, and said to Barney, "Knowing you were coming, and knowing what I was going to tell you, I did a little homework and found this. When *Huckleberry Finn* was first published, some libraries would not let it in because they said it was coarse. So Mr. Twain said this in response." Mrs. Salters read from the slip of paper:

" 'The truth is that when a library expels a book of mine and leaves an unexpurgated Bible around where unprotected youth . . . can get hold of it, the deep unconscious irony of it delights me. . . .'

"Here." She handed Barney the slip of paper. "It might fit into your story."

"So what happened?" Barney asked. "Did you save Mr. Dickens?"

"Finally," she said, "Mr. Moore and I came to an agreement. Mr. Dickens would stay on the open shelves, the Bible would stay on the open shelves, and I would stay as librarian. And neither of us would say a word about what had happened. So long as I kept silent, I could keep my job. But then Mr. Moore had his revenge. From that moment on, he told me, he would personally scrutinize every single book and magazine I ordered. And he would interrogate me about anything 'questionable' in any of them. He has the ultimate responsibility, he reminded me, for everything that comes into the school."

"You'd have to be on guard all the time," Barney said sympathetically.

"Indeed. I would have hundreds and hundreds of mean little conferences with him to look forward to. By forcing me to justify every piece of material I ordered, he'd make every day a torture for me. And as if that weren't punishment enough for my defying him, as he put it, Mr. Moore swore he would keep book on me."

"I don't understand," Barney said.

"That means," Karen Salters answered, "that he would keep a record of every time I was late, even by a couple of minutes; every form I made out that wasn't filled in exactly according to the rules; every complaint by a teacher that certain books had not yet arrived in the library even though I had ordered them in plenty of time, so it wasn't my fault. And on and on. I was to be constantly under suspicion. And he thought he could play this sadistic game as long as he liked because I wanted to stay in the job so much."

Karen Salters looked out the window and said softly, "I would have killed him if I'd stayed. One morning, sooner rather than later, I would have taken a butcher's knife, hid it under my coat, gone straight to his office as soon as I got to school, and cut out his tin heart. So although it did hurt terribly to leave my school, my library, I began to plan my departure. After all, I had restored the honor of Mr. Dickens, and that had been my main concern. I worked out a second agreement with Mr. Moore. I would leave voluntarily, and he would give me excellent recommendations—which I deserved—for any librarian's position I tried to obtain. In turn, I would continue to say nothing of how Mr. Moore had been persuaded to keep Mr. Dickens on the open shelves. Nor would I say anything of his having defaced a Bible, or anything about his little hidden censorship deals in the past—in which I, to my shame, had been a collaborator."

"But now"—Barney looked at her—"you're—"

"I am breaking the agreement. Obviously. Young man, I will not see my library, or what used to be my library, desecrated any longer. I was wrong. Even to save Mr. Dickens, I was wrong to keep silent. And I was inexcusably wrong to keep silent in order to save myself. Now it's *Huckleberry Finn*. Who knows what book it will be next week or next month? If this keeps on, in time there will be more closed than open shelves in our library. That's why I want people to know my story while there is still time."

"What's going to happen to you?" Barney frowned at his notebook.

"Oh," Karen Salters said, "Mr. Moore is now free, of course, to break his part of the agreement with me. He can contact my new employer, take back his letter of recommendation, and write a new one. A letter of *un*-recommendation. And that could lose me my new job before I ever start it. It's a risk I'll have to take."

"Yeah"—Barney suddenly looked cheerful—"but after your story comes out, I mean, if it's picked up by the regular papers, you'll be a kind of hero. Or heroine."

"I wouldn't want to take a vote on that, either," she said. "One thing is sure, I'll be controversial. And if you have figured in a controversy, even if you come out of it a heroine to some people, many employers look at you as if you have the bubonic plague. However, I have no choice in this matter. I *am* a librarian. So write it strong, young man, and write it accurate."

XIV

Mr. Moore waved Barney and Maggie Crowley to chairs across from his desk. The principal remained standing.

"You cannot print this interview with Karen Salters." Moore threw a manuscript on the desk.

"Is it untrue?" Barney asked.

"It would cause this high school to be held up to ridicule." Moore glared at the boy.

Barney looked at Maggie Crowley, who looked straight ahead as the principal continued. "Whatever the private and privileged communications were between me and my former librarian, what counts is that our disagreement—or, rather, misunderstanding—was resolved. Neither of the books in question was taken off the open shelves. Therefore, there is no story."

"Isn't it up to the editor," Barney said, "to decide what is newsworthy and what isn't?"

"Within certain guidelines set by this school." The principal's voice seemed to be coming from his teeth.

"Well, let's see," said Barney. "According to the guidelines, we can't print anything obscene. Is the story obscene?"

"Not in a technical sense," Moore said coldly.

"Okay." Barney's voice was a lot calmer than Barney was. "We also can't print anything libelous. Is this story libelous, Mr. Moore?"

"I just told you," Moore said. "It holds the school up to ridicule, and it holds *me* up to ridicule."

"But even if a story holds someone up to ridicule," Barney said, "it's libelous only if it's not true. You haven't answered my question about that, sir. Are you saying this story is untrue?"

"I am saying"—Mr. Moore rose and stood in front of the wall of photographs—"that it will harm the school."

"But this is a *public school* newspaper, sir," Barney said, "and we can't be censored for printing something controversial—unless it's obscene or libelous."

"If I want a legal opinion," Mr. Moore snapped, "I'll go to a lawyer, not a schoolboy."

Barney, who had been taking notes of what the principal was saying—to the clear displeasure of Mr. Moore—looked down at a sheet of paper on his lap. "There *is* one other justification for you to stop an article, according to the guidelines." He picked up the sheet and read: " 'Nothing may be published that would materially disrupt the classwork in this school or would otherwise create disorder or infringe upon the rights of others.' Do you believe that publishing this story would do any of those things?"

"It certainly infringes upon *my* rights, young man." Moore waved a finger at Barney.

"Would you tell me just how it does that, sir?" Barney said smoothly.

"Enough!" Moore roared. "This story is not to appear. Is that absolutely clear, Miss Crowley?"

Maggie Crowley, who had been listening to the exchange between Barney and the principal with the faintest of smiles, now looked solemnly at Mr. Moore. "Barney had a perfect right to ask those questions. According to the guidelines for the *Standard*—which, as you know, reflect the current state of the law on these matters—school authorities have no control over what is printed in a school paper except when the specific restrictions Barney asked you about are violated. And in this story, not a single one of them has been violated."

"Miss Crowley—" Moore started to growl warningly.

"The case of *Huckleberry Finn*," she continued, "has bitterly divided this community. Not only the school community but the town as well. The story Barney wrote is something everybody should know about before the final decision is made. It provides some valuable history that will help people get a clearer perspective on the issue."

"Miss Crowley—" The principal was growling again.

"Mr. Moore," she sailed on, "there comes a time when nothing is more important than self-respect. Nothing. I will not, I cannot, be any part of killing this story."

"Your resignation as faculty adviser is accepted," the principal said icily. "The story is dead."

Maggie Crowley got up from her chair. "No, it is not. I have a friend on the *Daily Tribune*."

"I AM NOT GOING TO BE BLACKMAILED TWICE!" Moore shouted. "FIRST BY THAT SALTERS WOMAN AND NOW BY THE TWO OF YOU."

"I do not consider it blackmail to use my First Amendment rights to help disseminate the news." Maggie Crowley's hands were shaking slightly. "And I suggest to you, sir, that you consider whether you want *two* stories circulating about your activities as a censor. Karen Salters's story, and then your attempt right now to kill her story."

Moore rubbed his chin. And rubbed it again.

"Of course, you can have space to reply to Mrs. Salters, sir," Barney said.

"You're a very smart lad," the principal said sourly. "Too smart for your own good." He turned to Maggie Crowley. "I'm going to have to think about this."

"We go to press tomorrow," she said.

The principal turned his back to them, and they left his office.

"What do you think?" Barney asked outside.

"I dunno." Maggie Crowley pushed her eyeglasses onto her hair. "If nothing else, he's got a lot of cunning. I think I got to him about how he'd look censoring a story about him being a censor. Of course, he could panic and come on like King Kong, but that's not his style. The one thing I do know for sure is that you and I have made a true enemy. But then, Barney, that's the best way to know the kind of person you are—by how rotten your enemies are."

Two days later, Barney's interview with Karen Salters appeared in the George Mason *Standard*. From the start of the school day, the principal's secretary, Rena Dwyer, told all inquirers that Mr. Moore was in conference. And she had no idea when he would be available for comment.

"Who's he in conference with?" Barney asked Maggie Crowley in her office early that afternoon.

"With himself," she said. "That's what Rena told me. He even had his lunch sent up from the cafeteria. I suppose he's still trying to figure out what to say."

Barney could hardly keep his eyes off the page of the *Standard* with the interview and the photograph of the school's former librarian. "I still don't understand," he said, "why we didn't hear from Mr. Moore again. He just let us go ahead and print without saying anything."

"What could he do, Barney?" Maggie Crowley leaned back in her chair. "He knew the story was going to get out anyway. I couldn't have been more clear about that. So what would he have gained by openly censoring something that was going to be out in the open anyway?"

"Well"—Barney sounded as if he were clearing his throat—"I guess the only thing he can do now is get back at *us*."

Maggie Crowley, looking at the window, sat up straight. "He won't have time to even think about that for a while. Here they come!"

Barney rushed over to the window and saw two television crews coming out of the parking lot with hand-held cameras and sound equipment. He made out the call letters of the two most popular channels in town, and leaning farther out the window, whooped in recognition of a reporter he had often seen on his set at home.

"I can see it already." Barney turned to Maggie Crowley. "They'll have a shot of Mighty Mike's closed office door."

"Oh," she said, "I think he'll find some time in his busy schedule to talk to them. If he stays behind that door all day, it's going to look as if he's ashamed to come out."

"I'm going down!" Barney said.

"They'll find you." Maggie smiled as she took a lipstick from her purse. "But go ahead if you like."

"Miss Crowley," he said at the door, "do you think this is going to be a national story?"

"I wouldn't be surprised," she said. "I think this is a first. The Holy Bible under suspicion, along with such a known felon as Huck Finn. You may be all over the map, Barney. By the way, you might tie your shoelaces."

That evening, Barney's father, leaning forward and grinning, watched the television interview with Barney. His mother was saying softly to the Barney who was on the screen, "That's right. You said it just right. Lost your comb again, I see."

Then Mr. Moore filled the screen. Calm, smiling amiably, he spoke of the precious American heritage of free speech and free press—reaching all the way from George Mason himself to the school proudly bearing his name.

"Of course, I did not for a moment contemplate even the merest notion that this article could not be printed," Moore told the interviewer. "This is America, is it not? How fortunate we all are that we live under a system that encourages the clash of ideas and opinions so that each of us can determine for himself or herself who is speaking the truth, and who is not."

"What a liar!" Barney said to the TV set.

"Shush," said his mother.

"But what about the charges made against you in the article?" the television reporter asked the principal. "That you have been censoring books behind the scenes for several years. That you wanted to take a Charles Dickens novel off the shelves. That you were even considering ripping out pages from the Bible, and that, as a matter of fact, you did tear out a section from one Bible in the school library."

Mr. Moore had the smile of a newborn babe. "As I said, it is only in the open marketplace of free speech that the truth will prevail, and so I am delighted beyond measure to have this chance to answer your incisive questions. These charges, as you put it, come from a woman, a decent woman, who misinterpreted certain things I may have said and came to erroneous conclusions. This was not malicious on her part. She is devoted to books, perhaps so passionately devoted to them that the people and events in those books are more real to her than the constantly complex flow of real life."

The principal's smooth voice grew deeper. "But I do not hold anything she has said against her. Not at all. All of us, at one time or another, jump to mistaken conclusions; and I have every expectation that eventually my dear friend Mrs. Salters will remember these events of the past much more accurately. In any case, I certainly wish her well in all her future endeavors."

"But, Mr. Moore," the television reporter persisted, "in what *specific* respects are her charges against you inaccurate?"

The principal smiled even more benignly. "I do not think that this is the time or the place for me to embarrass that good woman. No, I prefer to stand on my record of devotion to the First Amendment and to our school as the sanctuary of free inquiry."

"But, Mr. Moore," the reporter continued, "are you saying that nothing Mrs. Salters accuses you of actually happened?"

"Young man"—Mr. Moore sighed—"this has been a hard day for Mrs. Salters. She is not accustomed to being in the public eye, and so—"

"She did refuse to be interviewed on camera." The

reporter nodded. "In fact, I understand she will give no interviews at all. All she'd say on the phone is that she had told your school reporter all there is to tell, and there was nothing more to add."

"Yes, yes." Mr. Moore sighed again. "This is all too much for her, and I surely do not want to place any more of a burden on my old friend than she has already placed on herself."

A commercial came on.

"I can't believe this!" Barney said to his parents. "He got himself out of it like he was cutting butter. That reporter didn't lay a hand on him. Only poor Mrs. Salters got hurt. Mr. Moore made it sound as if she was sorry she'd said anything in the first place. As if *she* was a liar."

"Why do you suppose she's not giving any interviews?" Barney's father asked mildly.

"I'm not sure," the boy said. "I guess maybe Mr. Moore is right—she's not used to all of this. And I guess she does feel she has nothing more to say. Dad, do you think he'll get away with acting as if none of it ever happened?"

"Nope," his father said. "He smiles too much when he lies. It's like he's giving a commercial, and after a while, nobody believes those people. Besides, it's going to get to the folks around here that Moore isn't really answering Karen Salters's charges. So then you begin to figure: Why is that? Well, either the charges are true or they're not. So it follows that he's not answering her charges because they're true. An honest man would get angry and say she's a liar. But Moore can't do that because he knows that if he does call her a liar, she'll sue him—and win. Folks around here aren't stupid. They'll see through that unctuous hypocrite."

"Maybe," said Barney's mother. "Or else they'll run that unctuous hypocrite for Congress."

On two other channels that night, Barney saw Mr. Moore magnanimously pardon Karen Salters in practically the same silken words as on the early news.

He also watched Carl McLean state bluntly that whatever had happened at George Mason High School in the past—and he was in no position to judge the merits, one way or the other, of Karen Salters's story— nothing had changed with regard to the present confrontation about *Huckleberry Finn*. The review committee's decision was unsatisfactory, McLean said, in that it did not remove the book, root and branch, from the school. It would not do to keep the book on a restricted shelf. Racism, even on a restricted shelf, is infectious. The school board must do the decent, democratic thing and close off every avenue of access to *Huckleberry Finn* at George Mason and then at all our other schools.

The next day, Barney's story in the school paper— along with follow-up interviews with Mr. Moore and Mr. McLean, among others—dominated the local news in the *Daily Tribune*. During the next few days, much of the *Tribune*'s letters page was also devoted to a fiery debate over whether books can actually harm students

and, if so, which books. In addition, there were some
readers who asked, with varying degrees of sarcasm,
what lesson was being taught to young people by censoring what they can read.

"I can only conclude," said one such letter writer,
"that we are preparing our students for the Russians'
eventual take-over of this country."

A slight majority of the letters, however, supported
constant surveillance of school books. And a goodly
number of citizens commended Mr. Moore—with regard to the charges of past censorship by him—for
having had the courage to see that his students were
exposed only to books that would keep them healthy
in mind and body. That way, as adults, they would have
the strength of will and clarity of mind to resist the
insidious aggression of Communist ideas.

Within three days, television crews from NBC and
CBS were in town. For some weeks, both networks had
been preparing reports on the censorship wars in public
schools around the country; and when Barney's story
about Karen Salters was picked up by the wire services
—thereby appearing in newspapers in New York, Los
Angeles, and other cities—NBC and CBS came to an
identical conclusion. George Mason High School was
essential to their forthcoming reports. As one network
news official said to a correspondent. "It's as if Mark
Twain had written the script."

At this point, ABC's *Nightline,* a half-hour late-
evening news program, also decided to descend on the
high school. And once more, Mr. Moore smilingly for-

gave his critics; Mr. McLean spoke forcefully about the vicious effects of stereotyping black people; and Barney said that if students were to be deprived of a true American classic like *Huckleberry Finn,* not a single other book would be safe. Including, he added solemnly, the Bible.

"Are you a regular reader of the Bible?" *Nightline*'s host asked.

Barney paused. "Not as regular as I ought to be, sir. I just hope I won't be told I can't read it now."

The interviewer looked at Barney quizzically. "Who would tell you that?"

"Well," Barney said, looking worried, "since Mr. Moore was thinking the Bible ought to be censored, I don't know if my parents would want me to be reading it."

"WHAT!" Barney's father, watching in the living room, exploded.

"What a *terrible* thing to say!" Barney's mother was shaking her head. "My God, he's made us look stupid! Clear across the country! *Us!*"

When Barney came home from the studio a half hour later, his father moved to the door as soon as he heard Barney coming up the steps. "What the hell do you mean we won't let you read the Bible?" Mr. Roth said.

Barney's face reddened. "Gee, it just seemed a good thing to say right then. You know, to show that once a book is in trouble in school, it's in trouble everywhere."

"This is not everywhere," Barney's father said angrily. "You're getting to be like Mr. Moore. Point a camera at you and you lie."

"I still can't believe what I heard," Barney's mother said. "I've never been so shocked in my life. My own son making a fool out of me—on national television."

"I'm sorry," Barney said sheepishly. "I'm terribly sorry. It was a dumb thing to do. I was just thinking of scoring a point. I want us to win. But I really wasn't thinking at all. I won't do anything like that again."

"I hope so," his father said. "I wouldn't like to see a stranger take your place."

The next evening, on the state's public television network, Kate appeared on the set in the Roths' living room. She looked so crisp and so damn passionate, Barney thought, as she said, "Freedom is a seductive word, and it can be such a dangerous word. In the name of freedom of thought, should schools be allowed to put poison in children's minds by making them prejudiced against blacks or Jews or Orientals? Does freedom of thought mean that in a school *anything* can be said by a teacher? Does it mean that *anything* can be said in a book that is to be used in school?

"If schools don't teach what is right"—Kate looked right into the camera—"then what are they for? And if they are supposed to teach what is right, then, of course, they *must* have the authority to say that certain books are wrong and harmful and cannot be allowed in the classrooms and the library. You may call that censorship, I suppose, but then you're playing with words."

Kate then looked at the host of the program. "Would *you* be allowed to insult and humiliate black people on this show?"

The host tried a smile. "It's not a question of being allowed to. I wouldn't do it."

"Would you be *allowed* to?" Kate persisted.

"Well," the host said, "it is certainly not the policy of this—"

"Then why should it be the policy of George Mason High School?"

"Oh, God!" Barney groaned. "She's so damned smart."

"I trust that's not meant as a compliment," his father said.

Toward the end of the program, Deirdre Fitzgerald appeared on screen. Slumped in her chair, she looked tired, but when asked to respond to Kate's charge that freedom can be dangerous, Deirdre sat up straight, abruptly brushed the hair out of her eyes, and said:

"Oh, of course, freedom can be dangerous. It *is* dangerous. But the alternative is worse, far worse. Look at all the countries around the world where the people are told by their government what they can say and what they can read, and what they can't. All the countries where people are afraid that their very inner thoughts might become known and get them into terrible trouble.

"It was to prevent us from ever being in that state of despair and bondage"—Deirdre's voice was low and intense—"that those who created this nation chose freedom. With all of its dangers. And do you know the riskiest part of that choice they made? They actually believed that we could be trusted to make up our own minds in all the whirl of differing ideas. That we could be trusted to remain free, even when there were very, very seductive voices—taking advantage of our freedom of speech—who were trying to turn this country into the kind of place where the government *could* tell you what you can and cannot read. And their faith has been justified—the faith of those people who wrote and voted for the Constitution and the Bill of Rights. We still are free. And that's what this fight is all about. Are we going to stay free?"

"But what about that young woman's statement," the interviewer asked, "that schools exist in order to teach what is right, not what is wrong, and that therefore some books do not belong in a school? Even if this means restricting freedom?"

Deirdre Fitzgerald leaned forward. "I believe that all ideas, no matter how outrageous or unpopular, should be explored in a high school—"

"Oh," said the interviewer, "you *would* censor books in an elementary school?"

"I would use my head," Deirdre said. "I'm really not a nut, you know. I wouldn't give a second-grader calculus and I wouldn't give her a book by Judy Blume. Not all of her books anyway. But by high school, students should be examining all kinds of ideas if their education is supposed to be preparing them for the outside world. But this doesn't mean that the ideas being explored are to go unanswered.

"Earlier in this program," Deirdre went on, "Kate was saying that the state must teach what is *right* and therefore must exclude from the classroom and the library all ideas that are *wrong*, that might poison students' minds. Well, with all respect to Kate, this is the educational philosophy of dictatorships. It must not be ours. In our system, it should not be the role of teachers or librarians or principals to restrict ideas but rather to illuminate and analyze them, good and bad, so that students learn how to do that for themselves for the rest of their lives. I mean, so that students will learn how to think for themselves. *That* is teaching what's *right,* because it's teaching independence of thought."

"Tell that woman"—Barney's father, looking at the screen, said—"that she's letting us down as a librarian."

"What!" Barney was outraged.

"That's right. That woman ought to be running for President. Of the country, I mean."

XV

After all the coverage on television and on the wire services, the troubles at George Mason High School continued to be a national story—in the news magazines, on National Public Radio, and in daily newspapers where syndicated columnists warred with each other on the issue. Some insisted that a community had every right—through its elected school board—to insist that the values of the majority of the people living there be taught in the classrooms and be reflected in the books in the school. And that anything contrary to those values could properly be kept out of those schools. If the majority found *Huckleberry Finn* offensive for any reason, out he should go.

Others countered that while, of course, local public schools should teach the values of the local community, they should not exclude all other viewpoints from the library and the classrooms. To do that would be to impose an un-American orthodoxy of ideas on the students—let alone on the teachers and librarians. And one columnist quoted a Supreme Court justice: "The nation's future depends upon leaders trained [as students] through wide exposure to the robust exchange of ideas which discovers truth 'out of a multitude of tongues.'"

In many cities and states, moreover, call-in radio shows were also ablaze with listeners hooting at the very notion of censoring the Bible and *Huckleberry Finn* while other listeners—inspired, they said, by what was happening at George Mason High School—pledged themselves to start a crusade that would clean up the public school classrooms and libraries where *they* lived.

Back at the center of the storm, while the townspeople had at first enjoyed all the attention from outsiders, there was soon a growing sense of discomfort and embarrassment at being under this particular kind of national scrutiny.

"It's very distressing," Reuben Forster, chairman of the school board, said to his wife one evening. "We must look like a bunch of flatheads to the rest of the country. From now on, people will think of this town as the place where they arrest books."

"Come now," his wife said, "you're exaggerating terribly. You can't arrest a book!"

Reuben Forster put his pipe down because it was giving him no pleasure. "I've been thinking about this a good deal, my dear. Once a book is not allowed to circulate freely, once a book cannot move freely from one reader to another, it's just as if the book had been arrested and had its liberty curtailed. It's all very distressing. How are we going to get new businesses, new plants, to come here if we look as if we're some backwater village from the nineteenth century?"

The *Daily Tribune,* in a series of editorials, took a similar view. "There is a difference between publicity and notoriety," one of the editorials said, "and this town is becoming notorious wherever anybody can read. We're getting a reputation for narrow-mindedness that is going to make us the laughingstock of the country unless we do something about it."

Not all the townspeople, by any means, agreed with the editorial writer; but many of them did. In the letters column of the *Tribune,* there was now a clear, rising increase in the proportion of readers who wanted no action taken against Huck Finn. Wrote one indignant citizen: "If I want *my* child to study *Huckleberry Finn* in school, where are *my* rights as a free American citizen when some group of vigilantes acts to limit access to the book not only to their own children but to *all* kids at George Mason High School?"

Three days before the school board meeting on the fate of Huck Finn, the *Tribune* featured on its front page a letter from its managing editor, Sandy Wicks, who had been part of the majority of four in the review committee decision to keep *Huckleberry Finn* under guard in the high school.

Sandy Wicks wrote that she had, of course, been paying close attention to the views of the *Tribune*'s readers. And on rereading the book, she had decided that in view of the superior quality of the teachers and students at George Mason, she had now come to the conclusion that the true antibigotry message of *Huckleberry Finn* would come through clearly in the classrooms and in the library. There was no need to restrict the book.

She wished, Wicks added, that she could change her review-committee vote, but that was not possible under the rules of procedure. However, she hoped the school board would take her change of mind into consideration.

"Humph," Nora Baines said to Deirdre Fitzgerald as she tossed the *Daily Tribune* onto a chair. "Where was she when we needed her?"

"Oh, this will help," Deirdre said. "And I hear—though I don't know for sure—that Helen Cook and Frank Sylvester may co-sign a similar letter to the *Tribune*. Do you know that some of the other faculty members have not been speaking to them?"

"I do indeed." Nora smiled. "I am one of them. Traitors is what they are. How can a teacher approve locking up a book?"

Deirdre laughed. "You're a regular avenger. I can't do that, you know. I can't stop speaking to people because I don't agree with them. How can you be for a free exchange of ideas if you shut off dialogue just because you don't like what the other person is saying?"

"Stuff and nonsense," Nora Baines said. "Freedom of speech also means you have the right not to speak."

"You're evading my point, Nora," Deirdre said.

" 'I am what I am,' said Popeye the Sailor Man," Nora Baines explained.

"Okay." Deirdre grinned. "That puts an effective end to any attempt at logic in this discussion. Nora, I'm beginning to be optimistic about the school board vote. I think Huck's going to come out all right."

"If you're right," Nora said, "this will bear out the Baines Theory of Battle Against the Forces of Darkness."

"And that theory is?"

"Well," Nora said, "we are the forces of light, right?"

"Shining all the time," Deirdre said.

"Therefore, the more light we keep getting on our side, the stronger we are. Therefore, the way to fight censorship—not only here, but anywhere—is to let the whole story hang out, from the moment of the first attack, so that it gets in the papers and on television and on radio. Again and again and again. The reason Mighty Mike got away with locking up books before is that he did it in the dark. Nobody on the outside knew anything about it. That's what I hope school people all around the country are going to learn from this. The censors can't stand light. Any more than Dracula could stand the cross."

In his office at We-Have-It-All headquarters, Reuben Forster was engaged in an intense dialogue with himself.

"I hear"—one voice was scratchy—"that they're going to have someone dressed as Mark Twain come and speak for Huck Finn at the school board meeting. They say it'll look great on television around the country."

"I will not allow it," Reuben Forster said in his own voice, as forcefully as he could. "Mr. Twain is not a member of this community. He does not pay taxes here."

"Oh, they'd love that." The scratchy voice went into a cackle. "Mark Twain thrown out of a school board meeting for speaking on behalf of free speech! What'll you do if he won't leave? Throw him in the jug? Hee-hee-hee."

"Well, I'd not be having Mark Twain arrested. I'd be having some real person arrested for disturbing the peace."

"That's not the way it will look on the network news," the other voice said. "It would be Mark Twain dragged away by the cops and put in jail right alongside his book."

Reuben Forster now sounded conciliatory. "Do you suppose Mr. Twain might not come if he was told his presence would not be necessary? If he was told there's no chance of any harm coming to his book? I happen to have information to that effect."

"Maybe he'd decide to stay away," said the scratchy voice. "But why should he believe you?"

"Now see here!" Forster was so angry that his teeth cracked the stem of his pipe. "Everybody knows I am a man of my word."

"Even the dead?" The cackle had started again. "Do even the dead know that?"

"You're mixing me up," the chairman of the school board said.

"I'll tell you what," said the scratchy voice. "If you can get word out that he doesn't have to worry about what's going to happen to Huck, then maybe Mr. Twain might decide not to make the trip from wherever he is at present."

Reuben Forster lit his pipe, walked around the room, walked around again, and then opened the door. "Would you get Mr. Moore on the phone," he said to his secretary. "Tell him I want to see him right away. Fast as he can get here."

Fifteen minutes later, the principal, smiling, entered the office, took a seat, and waited.

"Thank you for coming," Mr. Forster said. "Informally, and therefore quite unofficially, I have taken a straw vote of the board. By a substantial majority, it would appear, the board tomorrow night will overturn the decision of the review committee."

"Well, between me and you, Mr. Forster," Moore said, "I thought the review committee was too soft. Of course, it'll cause a lot of fuss, banning the book outright, but we can handle it. And I think in the long run, the board will win a lot of deserved respect for not giving in to all this emotional propaganda that's been going on about so-called censorship. Our responsibility, after all, is to the youngsters and not to—"

"You misunderstand me, Mr. Moore." Reuben Forster started to fill his pipe. "The majority of the board appears to be of a mind to place no restrictions whatsoever on the use of *Huckleberry Finn* in class or in the library."

There was just the slightest blink before Mr. Moore said, smiling broadly, "Very well. The board is boss."

"Indeed." Reuben Forster nodded. "Also, after the open meeting, it is my sense that the board would like to have a closed session with you in a few days."

"May I ask the nature of the agenda?"

"That interview in the school paper with Mrs. Salters," the chairman said. "We think it's time to review your policies, your *informal* policies, concerning the removal of books from the curriculum and from the open shelves of the school library. I can even give you a little preview of what the board has on its mind for the future. From now on, the board will want to be informed of *all* complaints concerning books and other materials—whether made formally or not. And we will want to know how each one of them is handled. The board intends to avoid any possibility of censorship behind closed doors."

Mr. Moore kept on smiling. "The board has only to decree, and I shall obey. But as for the review, once all of you see the full record, you will realize that Mrs. Salters did not choose to give all the facts."

"We shall see." Reuben Forster had yet to return Mr. Moore's smile. "Oh, there's another thing, Moore.

Have you taken, or do you intend to take, any reprisals against Mrs. Salters because of what she said about you in that interview?"

"Why, my goodness," Mr. Moore said, "such a thing never occurred to me, never could occur to me."

Reuben Forster knocked the ashes out of his pipe. "You are not under oath, Mr. Moore, but I expect the truth. There has been no recent communication between you and her new employers?"

"Not yet. I mean, of course not. I wrote an enthusiastic recommendation for Mrs. Salters some months ago, and I have neither added to nor detracted from it since."

"So"—Forster pointed the stem of his pipe at Mr. Moore—"there is not the slightest possibility that we on the board will ever hear of any *second* letter from you to Mrs. Salters's new employer?"

"Not the slightest possibility," the principal said with great sincerity.

"One last thing." Reuben Forster rose from his seat behind the desk. "What I have just told you about the straw vote indicating the board's ruling tomorrow night—"

"Yes?"

"That information is to go no farther than this room."

"Of course." The principal nodded his head vigorously.

The two shook hands, and Mr. Moore left.

Sitting back in his black leather chair, Reuben Forster looked benignly at the ceiling.

"The best way," he purred, "the very best way to spread a piece of news is to make it confidential. Especially to someone like Moore who always likes to appear as if he's on the inside of every little thing. I really do dislike that man. I must check the expiration date of his contract."

XVI

The school board meeting, originally scheduled for the George Mason High School auditorium, was transferred to the considerably larger town hall. Leaning forward in his seat at the center of the stage a short time before the meeting was to begin, Reuben Forster dearly wished he could have banned all the television cameras. But since this was a public meeting, he didn't see how he could do that without looking as if he and the board were hiding something.

Then, as he watched one crew testing its sound equipment, Forster brightened. Since he was quite certain how the vote was going to come out, it *was* a good thing the television cameras were there. Now the town would no longer be laughed at around the country as the place where even the Bible could get into trouble.

It looked as if most of the people in town had come. So many, in fact, that the overflow had to be directed to a smaller meeting room where the proceedings would be shown on closed-circuit television.

"What's the point of coming?" said a disgruntled citizen who had been shunted off to the auxiliary room along with his wife. "It's just the same as watching from home."

"Not if there's a good fistfight or two," his wife said cheerfully. "Then we could say we were right there."

But there were no fistfights. Indeed, since many of the speakers were the same ones who had been heard at the review-committee meeting, the level of passion was somewhat lower. Since they had heard each other before, each side knew the moves the opposition was going to make at just about every turn. Even the bursts of anger were predictable.

Carl McLean did get up and say he had heard the school board had already made up its mind, and he warned them against going against the wishes of the black parents and their allies in the community. "You may have come in here thinking you were going to vote one way," he said, pointing to the members of the board on stage, "but if you still want to be sitting there after the next election, you better start thinking again."

One of the relatively few new speakers was Steve Turney, the thin, bespectacled black student who had refused to join the walkout from Nora Baines's class that had been led by Gordon McLean in protest against the continued presence there of Huck Finn.

"I am a junior at George Mason High School,"

Turney said in a quick, clear voice, the rhythms of which were like that of a typewriter handled by a very assured typist. "I am here to speak for my right as a student not to have my education interfered with by people—well-meaning but uninformed people—outside the school. And I am here to speak for the same right for students who come after me.

"First of all," Turney went on, "I have read this book. I have read this book in its entirety. From what I have heard at this meeting, and at the other meeting in the school auditorium, I do not believe that all the people complaining about this book have read it all. If they had, and if they *can* read, they wouldn't have been saying what they said about it. Second, many of those complaining about this book say they want to protect *me,* as a black person, from certain words in this book. Well, it is too late to do that for *me.* I have already seen and heard those words. And since they are not new to me, and believe me they are not, I know when those words—I mean particularly 'nigger'—are directed at *me.*"

Turney paused and looked down at a slip of paper in his hand. "In this book, those words—particularly 'nigger'—are not intended by the author, Mr. Clemens, also known as Mark Twain, to insult or humiliate *me* or any other black person. They are clearly intended to rebuke and bring scorn to those ignorant, so-called grown-up white people in the book who use those words."

"Huckleberry Finn himself uses 'nigger' all the time, young man!" Carl McLean shouted from the first row.

"Yes," Steve Turney said calmly. "Yes, he does. And that is what makes this book so interesting. Huckleberry Finn uses that word because the way he grew up, and where he grew up, it was the natural thing to do. A lot of evil comes natural, sir. That's why it's so hard to overcome evil in oneself. But Huckleberry Finn, he doesn't *feel* or mean the word 'nigger' the way the white grown-ups do. He doesn't *see* black people as niggers, even though he does use the word. He sees Jim as a *man,* a man who should be free, and he tries hard to help keep him free.

"I think"—Steve Turney looked around the hall— "this book has a lot to teach *everybody,* even though it was written so many years ago. What it teaches is that a boy can be better, a whole lot better, than what he's been taught to be. A lot of young people still need to be shown that. In this town too. At our school too.

"With all respect to everybody on the other side"— Turney was now speaking quite slowly—"I think it is dumb to punish this book in any way. If I were principal of my school, I would make sure that every single student read this book before leaving my school. That is all I have to say. Except that I feel I am very fortunate because nobody can protect me from this book anymore. Even if they burn this book, I have read it. And I will never forget this book."

Carl McLean rose to say that Steve Turney was a

sad, a poignant, example of a black child who had already been brainwashed by this book—so brainwashed that he did not even *know* when he was being insulted and stereotyped.

The debate went on and on, and Reuben Forster kept looking at his watch, trying to decide when to call for a vote. Noticing a whispered conference in the back of the room between Carl McLean and Matthew Griswold, Forster braced himself. The wind ain't going their way, he said to himself, so they're going to play for time so they can turn the wind around.

"Mr. Chairman! Mr. Chairman!" McLean was waving vigorously. "The hour is getting late, and I move that in view of the wise precedent set by the review committee at the last meeting on this issue—when they asked not to be hurried into a decision—that we provide the same courtesy to you and the rest of the school board this time. There is no urgent need for you to reach a decision tonight. Reflect for a day or a week on what you have heard this evening. And"—McLean's voice grew sharper—"reflect on the impact of your decision on your future in public office."

Reuben Forster felt for the cold pipe in his pocket. "Mr. McLean," the chairman of the school board said slowly, "I do believe we have *all* sufficiently reflected on this matter. However, I will ask the members of the board if they would like to take advantage of your considerate suggestion."

Forster looked up and down the table. No member of the board indicated a desire to reflect any longer.

"Well, then," the chairman said, "it's time to vote."

There was one vote to affirm the original judgment of the review committee that *Huckleberry Finn* be removed from all required classroom reading lists; that only certain students, with parental permission be given the book on optional reading lists; and that, in the school library, the book be kept on a restricted shelf to be read by a student only with the written permission of a teacher and a parent.

The other four members of the school board voted to free Huck Finn from any and all restrictions in the classrooms and the library of George Mason High School.

On the way out of the hall, Deirdre Fitzgerald was crying with relief. Smiling through her tears, she said to Nora Baines, "I just hope that after all this, Huck doesn't decide to run away and light out for the Indian territory. God, after what he's been put through, I wouldn't be surprised if he did just that."

The next morning, Mr. Moore was in early. If he was disappointed in the school board's decision, he showed no sign of it. Indeed, his secretary told Maggie Crowley later in the day that the principal was unusually cheerful.

"I can't figure it," Rena said. "*He* didn't win any victory. All along, he tried to make it look as if he wasn't on either side—just smack in the middle. And I happen to know"—Rena lowered her voice—"that the board wants to look into some of those charges that

Karen Salters made about his little censorship deals before all of this. So you tell me, why is Mighty Mike
going around acting like some rich relative died?"

"Beats me," Maggie Crowley said. "I bet you something tricky's going on in his teeny mind."

In his office, Mr. Moore was walking slowly, back
and forth, before the great wall of photographs. He
stopped in front of John Wayne's picture and gave it a
friendly rap with his knuckle.

"Duke," the principal said softly, very softly, "you
know and I know that most of the folks on the winning
side don't take this censorship stuff all that seriously.
Sure, a few of them do, but the rest, they got carried
away. Once all those TV cameras started coming
around, they didn't want to look like yokels. But there'll
be so many things on their minds between now and
the school board elections next year that this stuff about
the books will seem like ancient history.

"So"—Moore smiled—"if McLean, Griswold, and
the people with them do a smart, quiet job of organizing
—without blowing up this whole issue again but fixing
on some other grievances—they could elect a majority
of the board. Because the other side is going to think
they don't *have* to organize, they've already won. And
so a lot of them aren't even going to bother to vote.

"Well, now"—the principal broke briefly into what
looked like a jig—"that new school board would be
very happy with a principal who knows how to deal
with bad books the right way. A principal to whom

any member of the new majority of the board could come with a complaint about a book and know it'd be taken care of fast and sure. Yes, sir, and that kind of school board might want to make that kind of principal *superintendent* of schools."

Mr. Moore started to hum, and someone with an unusually acute musical ear might have been able to detect in the drone a badly bent trace of "Oh, What a Beautiful Morning."

"Now that it's all over," Barney said, "are we friends?"

Kate smiled. "It's not all over. Nothing's ever all over. That's what keeps me going."

"Some day we're all going to be all over," Luke said. "Do you at least concede that?"

"Some of us," Kate said, "will not be all over ever, because some of us will have left a mark, a contribution, on which new generations can build. And others of us"—Kate gave Luke a pitying smile—"will simply disappear, as if they had never been here."

"That mark *you're* going to leave"—Luke grinned back—"is that going to be a big 'T' and a big 'C' for Thought Control?"

"It's fascinating"—Kate turned to Barney—"to watch so primitive a mind try so hard to function. It's like *The Little Engine That Could.* Except *she* finally made it."

"*She?*" Luke slapped his thigh.

"Why is it," Kate said, "that a piece of machinery can be 'he' in the first place but you yelp like a hound-dog if it's referred to as 'she'?"

"Kate's got a point." Barney smiled.

"Maybe," Luke said. "But will Kate admit we scored some points, a hell of a lot of points, in the battle of Huck Finn?"

"You won, didn't you?" She looked at Luke.

"That's not what I mean," Luke said. "Did any of our points finally get through to *you*?"

"Steve Turney got through to me," Kate said as Barney listened intently. "When he told the school board he could tell when 'nigger' was meant for him. And that it *wasn't* meant for him in *Huckleberry Finn*. That bothered me. I thought I'd been fighting for Steve, for everybody black in the school. And here was this black person telling me to butt out of his business. And he wasn't playing to the white folks, either. Steve doesn't let anybody mess with him, you know that."

"So why didn't you say something after you heard Steve?" Barney asked.

"I had to think about it," Kate said. "I'm still not saying I've changed my mind entirely about that damn book. I'm just saying I'm a little less sure than I was. Anyway," she went on cheerfully, "it's all part of the learning process. So take heart, little engine." Kate patted Luke on the shoulder. "Your mind will grow too —as much as it can."

"So you're going to cool it a little from now on?" Luke said to her. "You're not just going to jump right into something—and wait until it's all over before you start thinking?"

"I'm going to jump *and* think, my friend, all at the same time." She poked Luke in the stomach. "That's the way I am."

"If you don't think before you jump," Barney said, "you could drown."

"Wherever have I heard that before?" Kate shook her head. "Actually, my grandfather had a twist to that. He once told me, 'When someone plunges in the sea and drowns, you can't blame the sea. You must learn to swim.' That's what I'm doing all the time. Swimming and thinking, thinking and swimming right along. The Little Activist That Could. Next time, I'll beat the socks off you guys."

"My, my, my," Mr. Moore's voice boomed behind them. "What do we have here? Sweet reconciliation— or is it only a truce?"

"It sure ain't surrender," Kate said brightly.

"Well, it's all behind us now." Mr. Moore smiled all around. "I'm sure there are no hard feelings."

"Against whom?" Barney said innocently.